Bad Boy

By

Jordan Silver

Table of Contents

Chapter 1

Chapter 2

Chapter 3

Chapter 4

Chapter 5

Chapter 6

Chapter 7

Chapter 8

Chapter 9

Chapter 10

Chapter 11

Chapter 12

Chapter 13

Chapter 14

Chapter 15

Chapter 16

Chapter 17

Chapter 18

Chapter 19

Chapter 20

Chapter 21

Chapter 22

Chapter 23

Chapter 24

Epilogue

Chapter 1

Jacqueline

I've had it with this shit. No more doormat, no more Ms. Goody Two Shoes. I picked up my phone from the mattress beside me. Only one person I know who will understand how I'm feeling without judging me. Without bringing up my past like a mallet to beat me over the head. One little slip in judgment when I was eighteen years old and I have to live like a nun forever. Well fuck that the habit's coming off. I'm lonely, horny and pissed the fuck off. No almost twenty two year old is supposed to feel like this.

I'm not a bad person. I mean I have done some fucked up things in my life but who haven't? So why does that one little mishap get to rule the rest of my life? Meanwhile Jake Summers gets to go on with life as usual.

So what I lost my cherry in the backseat of his mustang on the football field? Big deal. And so what if deputy Smalls caught us and made a big stink about it? So what if mommy and daddy had to hear about it along with half the town? Who then felt it necessary to spread it to the other half. That was four long years ago and I've decided that I've been punished enough.

Didn't I have to give up my scholarship and go to the local community college because momma and daddy forbid me to leave? Apparently getting your cherry popped by the town's bad boy in the backseat of his souped up ride was a taint on your character for the rest of your life. Not only that it was the gateway to hell to hear them tell it.

The only good thing about that whole deal was that I was able to finish my four-year degree in three. That'll happen when you've been cut off from the rest of the free world for three damn years.

Jake Summers. I still blush just

thinking about him.

He'd tried to contact me after that night but daddy had made threats, and since the sheriff was a good buddy of his, (more like daddy owned him) poor Jake had given up. But not without trying behind the scenes at least a couple more times.

He had left town a few days later, hadn't seen or heard from him in three years. His sister Mindy had kept in touch but we had to keep our friendship hidden. Daddy didn't want any reminders of my shame as he calls it.

Now Mindy has been badgering me about going out with her. She knows I'm not allowed but it doesn't stop her from trying every so often.

I like hanging out with Mindy, it makes me feel closer to her brother somehow though she never talks about him anymore.

In the beginning she'd brought him up every other second but when she realized how much it hurt me she'd stopped. I miss hearing about him but it was just too painful.

He was the only boy I'd ever loved. Well boy might be a bit of a stretch. He was twenty-three when I was eighteen. Rumor had it that he was smart but he was drawn to the dark side, fast cars and motorcycles.

When we met he'd just been home from college. It was hard to believe he'd actually been, he just didn't fit the profile. Leathers and tats did not spell alumnus if you know what I mean. But talking to him made me realize just how much you should never judge a book by its cover.

Jake was insightful and knowledgeable about a lot of things. Too bad that wasn't enough for daddy when the shit hit the fan. All he saw was a kid from the wrong side of the tracks who wasn't even good enough to walk in his little girl's shadow.

He'd run him off, the only man I'd ever felt for and in the last three years proceeded to parade the sorriest bunch of assholes this side of the Mississippi before me every chance he got. I fixed him though, fixed him good.

Every one of them went away knowing about my sin. I might embellish the truth a bit, saying that the incident had made the newspapers. And since most of them were mama's boys out to please they ran like a scalded cat. Daddy had fits but what could he do? He finally took note and stopped bringing them around about six months ago.

I don't know what's gotten into me. For all intents and purposes I've been cool with my lot. But now school was over. I can go out and make my own way. I'm no longer dependent on my parents to take care of me and by rights I'm a grown woman.

I want out. I refuse to spend another night reliving the heat and passion of my one encounter. When my kitty gets wet the next time I want there to be something more than memories to get me through. I wish I knew where Jake was right now.

Maybe I'll ask Mindy, maybe he would still be single and have been pining away for me the same way I've been yearning for him.

Yeah right. No one that looks like that can stay single for that long. Who am I kidding? My heart hurt just a little at the thought of it. But what did I expect? Jake had been a man when we met. A man who packed a punch even then, I could only imagine how much he'd improved with age, and experience.

Thoughts of my Jake with anyone else could usually send me into a melancholic haze for days on end. Those are the days I hated daddy most. I've cried enough tears over Jake Summers to flood the Mississippi and I'm sure before my life is done I'd cry even more. Because if there's one thing I know, there'll never be another like him for me.

I hadn't known him when he lived in the area before and was the school quarterback. He was five years ahead of me in school after all, and besides I never got to hang with the cool kids.

That summer when he'd been home for the last time I'd been tutoring his sister Mindy who is just a few months younger than I am. I'd taken one look at him that day when he came into her room where we'd been studying, and lost my heart.

Daddy had no idea who it was I was tutoring of course, or where it was. He would've had ten fits if he'd ever known. For him the pride that his beloved daughter had been chosen as a tutor her senior year was enough. And I guess he thought the school held to the same ideals as him and put like with like as he calls it. In that token he would never have expected them to pair his unblemished lily-white angel with someone of a lesser pedigree. As I've grown and matured I've come to realize that daddy is a heel.

I watched the lone mosquito flit around above my head and I tried to drum up the courage to make the call. If I did this there was no going back. I have never in my life defied daddy in anything. There's no doubt that he would hear about it if I went out on the town with the sister of the man he blames for my fall from grace.

There was a war going on inside me. I

could taste freedom on the tip of my tongue, but fear held me back. I don't have the first clue about being on my own. I've never had to fend for myself before. As the only child and daughter of Gary and Sandy Willoughby I have been pampered all my life. Daddy expects me to toe the line until the grave, which means following his every dictation.

Something I've done with the exception of that one night. That one fateful night that was the beginning and the end. He'd been so gentle, so kind. Nothing at all like the bad boy who spoke rough and gave me looks hot enough to destroy my panties in ten seconds flat. I must admit looking back I'd followed him around like a puppy all summer.

That first night watching him with his sister, the playful way they interacted with each other. Something sweet had unfurled inside me. I'd wanted that with him, wanted the attention.

Only when he'd turned his attention to me the intense heat in his gaze had been anything but brotherly. And when he smiled at me for the first time and his dimples were on full display, I knew he was going to be the father of my babies. My ovaries had spoken.

"Who's your friend Mindy?" His voice had been rough and smooth at the same time, which made no sense. All I know is that his sweet timber had sent shivers down my spine and since he'd said it while still staring at me like he wanted to eat me in the good way I was all but vibrating. Mindy had been giggling as he tickled her, school work forgotten at the sight of her big brother who'd come home for the summer.

"Oh sorry Jake this is Jacqueline we call her Jackie for short. Jackie this is my big brother Jake." I'd blushed bright pink and stuttered like a ninny, wishing the floor would open up and swallow me whole.

It was the first time I'd realized the effect my parents' strict upbringing had had on my existence. I had no social graces outside of eating with dignitaries at state dinners. In short I hadn't the first clue how to react in the social setting of boy meet girl. And this should not have been my first foray. He was way too much man for my little heart to take. I wanted.

"Hello Jacqueline." Was that my name? Was that the name my mother had given me? Why had it never sounded so sweet before? Why had I never had the urge to strip naked and present myself on a platter at the mere sound of it?

My soft reply was barely audible but it was all I could get pass the lump that was forming in my throat. I stood in that room near tears because even then I knew. He would never be mine. Whatever my heart was feeling at this moment it would be torn before the night was done.

I had no doubt that I would cry out that pain against my pillow. Daddy would never let me have him. That's even if he was interested which there wasn't a snowball's chance in hell of that happening. I'm green but I'm not that dense.

I have a fairly good understanding of how these things work and though I'm not blind to my own attributes, I do know that I'm nowhere near his caliber. Beautiful people usually leaned towards others of the same ilk. Not brunettes with brown eyes and hips that are just a little too wide.

I tried shaping them down but they have a mind of their own and though I'm a size eight there's no getting away from my ass and hips. No someone like him will end up with some super model type with long blonde hair and a perfect size two body. Someone whose daddy didn't run her life like a drill sergeant.

Chapter 2

Jake

"You seen my girl lately?"

"We talk."

"You tell her I'm coming back to that rinky dink town to get her and no one, not even her fuck of an old man is gonna stand in my way this time."

"Jake you can't just..."

"She's mine...tell her to get ready because I'm coming and when I leave she's on the back of my fucking bike." I hung up the phone and put it back in my pocket.

"Hector we done here? I've got shit to do."

"Cool it esse just a minute, I have to test the merchandise." The asshole snorted a line of the grade A powder in front of him while three armed men stood back from their boss who was watching from his place at the head of the table.

The old warehouse was musty and damp and I was over this shit already. I had everything I needed, all that's left was for me to tie this shit up and get on the road. I'd put in for three months leave, another smart move on my part. No vacation time in the past three years, and no sick leave. I'd wracked up my days for just this occasion.

I knew when I finally got my hands on her again it was going to take at least that long for me to feel like I'd put my stamp on her. I just needed these fucks to finish up this deal so I could burn their asses and be done with it.

There had been an influx of new crank coming into the US from Europe of all places. This shit made everything that came before it look like child's play. It was supposedly laced with some chemical that some twisted fuck in Russia concocted in a lab and was geared strictly towards the US. Talk about chemical warfare.

Whatever the shit was it was

spreading throughout the Midwest like wildfire, it was cheap, highly effective and in great supply.

There was only one draw back; the shit was lethal. After one hit you're hooked and within the week of over indulging your new high you ended up assed out in a rat hole somewhere. It also makes you crazy as fuck coming onto the end with the sweet little side bennie of a taste for human flesh. I wanted this shit off my streets yesterday.

"It's good Mikhail, excellent shit." Hector smiled at the Russian mob boss who in all the times we'd met had spoken maybe ten words. It had taken my task force months to set up this relationship. To foster it and nurture it until it was what it was today.

These criminal types aren't the most trusting fuckers in the world so gaining their trust takes some doing. It meant moving out of my nice comfortable condo and into a seedier side of town. It meant a whole new identity which was nothing new, I've done this shit too many times in the last three years to count, but this time my shit had to be tight.

This was no low level runt we were dealing with here, these ex KGB fucks are as crazy as they come and they know their shit. On our first meeting the fucker knew the whole history of my made up family. Dumb fuck. He might be good but I'm better. That's why the force had given me my own division when I signed up.

It didn't hurt that the Feds and the fucking kooks had come knocking, so when I chose to go with the city's PD instead they'd been only too happy to have me. I had the brainpower and they had the trainers to hone me into a fucking super killer. Now I felt ready. Ready to go take back what the fuck was mine.

Chapter 3

Jacqueline

I'm going to do it, no more stalling. Lately Mindy's been a lot more persistent than usual as if she were on a mission of some sort. She knew better than anyone else what my life was like. She also knew that there was only one thing that would fix what ailed me.

Tonight I'm going to ask her, tonight I'll find the courage to bring up his name and see what happens? With any luck she won't tell me that he's married and happy somewhere with some other woman. I rubbed my tummy where the dull ache begun, it was always that way whenever I thought of Jake with another girl, loving her the way he did me.

"I can't go on like this this is nuts." Jumping off my bed I headed for the door to assess the lay of the land. All was quiet out there but you never know where daddy might be lurking, he's weird like that. I tiptoed down the hallway to my parents' door and placed my ear against it. Please don't let them be doing anything but sleeping or in the middle of one of daddy's lectures. It seemed quiet in there so I headed back to my room.

Taking a deep breath I dialed Mindy who seemed to be waiting by the phone because she snatched it up on the first ring. "Please tell me you can break out of solitary girlfriend." I had to laugh at her description of my life, she wasn't too far off the mark.

Ever since I'd put the brakes on daddy's matchmaking attempts he's been holding me prisoner almost. That was his way of bending me to his will I guess. Little did he know that the only reason I'd been playing it safe for the past three and a half years was so I could one day be completely free of him and his tyrannical rules.

After I drag every bit of information out of Mindy about Jake I'm going to find him, that's my big plan. What happens after that is anybody's guess but at lease I would know that I'd tried for my happiness. "I'll meet you on the outskirts of town maybe we can go to that place you're always talking about."

"Are you serious? This is great, I have something to tell you but I don't want to do it over the phone…" She started rambling but I cut her off before she got too far, there's only one thing I wanted to know right now, the one thing that would decide the course of my actions. "Just answer me this one thing Mindy…is Jacob married?"

"No he isn't that's what I need to talk to you about." My whole body relaxed with her admission, I hadn't even been aware that I'd been that tense. As long as he was still free I could work with that, I just hope he even remembered me, or even wanted me still.

I had my first niggling of fearful doubt. What if he didn't want me anymore? What if all those things he'd whispered to me while he'd been thrusting himself into my body were just empty words? Things said to a naïve girl in the heat of the moment? No Jackie don't give up now, you've been waiting for this for far too long to give up now.

"We'll talk when I get there let me get dressed and I'll be out of here in half an hour. And Mindy I have something to tell you too." I'd never told her how I still felt about her brother and if I was going to pull this off I was going to need her help. I dug out the low rider jeans and black halter-top I'd buried at the bottom of my closet, and the three inch heeled snakeskin boots.

Daddy wouldn't approve but I just had to have them. I'd actually had Jake in mind when I bought them earlier in the year on one of my rare solo shopping trips. Mom usually took me shopping and then it was sundresses and skirts. Jeans apparently were for the lower classes; somebody forgot to tell daddy that he wasn't the king of Siam.

I checked myself out in the mirror. Not bad although my ass looked like it was trying to escape. The heels added a little height and lifted things rather nicely if I do say so myself. I wasn't sure about the cleavage I've never shown that much skin before, very daring. I felt my blood spike as I imagined Jake seeing me in something like this. When we'd been sneaking around three years ago all he'd ever seen me in were the little girl dresses mom insisted I wear. It was a wonder he'd even noticed me back then. But he had, boy had he ever.

Chapter 4

Jake

Three and a half years ago she was too young. I couldn't ask her to walk away from her family and everything she knew, it wouldn't have been fair. I know her asshole sperm donor thinks that he and his friends had scared me off but nothing could be farther from the truth. I'd already made up in my mind by then what I was going to do.

How I was going to bide my time until she was considered an adult in every sense of the word. I have everything all planned out, been planning since the first day she looked at me like I hung the fucking moon. I'm not stupid, I knew there was no way her old man would go for it but I also knew that what I saw in her eyes back then, and what I had begun to feel in my heart could overcome anything in time.

I hadn't meant to take her that night. We'd been sneaking around behind her father's back for weeks every chance we got. She'd given him and her mom some cockamamie story about extra tutoring, and they were so lax that they'd never given it another thought. I'd learned from our conversations that as long as her dad thought he was in control that's all he cared about.

He wasn't too much into the details, or maybe it was just that he'd cowed his wife and daughter so much over the years that he expected blind obedience in all things. I'd peeped his game from the gate that's why I'd been willing to wait. I know his type.

Having been born into poverty I knew what it felt like to be under everyone's thumb. People seemed to equate lack of money with lack of human feeling. If you're poor you were to be treated like trash.

Gary Willoughby was the worse sort of asshole when it came to that offense. I don't think he even knew what me or anyone else in my family looked like for that matter and my mother and father had worked for him for years before dad died.

I'd tried to get mom out after the whole

thing went down and he'd threatened to fire her but she'd refused. She didn't think her twenty three year old son should carry the burden of taking care of a mother and a younger sister. I was just getting my start in the force but even then I would've made it work.

I tuned back in to what was going on around me can't carry out an Op with a hard on which is my usual state whenever I think of my baby girl. Three, almost four years of going without pussy was playing hell on my dick but my boy didn't want anyone but her. Too bad for the criminal element, I used all my pent up energies and frustration hunting their asses.

"Let's finish this then if you're happy with the goods, the boss will be waiting." I passed him the case full of money, which he passed off to one of the goons to be checked for authenticity.

This shit was nothing like the movies. It took time and planning to be executed just right. These fucks took their business seriously, down to every last detail and they had the money and resources to carry it out.

This fuck Mikhail Zubrinsky could buy and sell three third world countries and still be a multi billionaire. Why the fuck he needed to get caught up in this shit was anyone's guess but I guess once an agent always an agent.

It had been fun pitting my skills against the best The Rus had to offer. They thought they were so slick, thought they were getting one over on the good old U.S. of A but they were fucked.

Even now as we speak the rest of my team was busy rounding up his lackeys. His front man had been the first to go down, then the assholes that'd been peddling this shit from Kansas to Texas.

We had the Mexicans pushing weed on one side and these fucks coming in from the other. The Chicanos had a new problem now though. They were no longer high on the D.E.A.'s list of takedowns but since America had jumped on the legalization bandwagon our shit was homegrown; they were fucked.

Chapter 5

Jake

I saw the goon nod his approval to his boss and sent my signal to my team that had the place surrounded. There was a flurry of movement as the door was broken down and the place flooded with undercover cops with guns drawn.

"Nobody move, hands in the air." I kept my eyes on Mikhail as I raised my hands in surrender, one wrong move and I would have no problem blowing my cover to put a cap in his ass.

"What the fuck what is this? You narced me Zubrinsky you fuck?" Hector flew at the other man who even under threat of arrest was one smooth customer. He got up from the table as one of the agents restrained Hector.

Folding his arms across his chest he looked down his nose at the rest of us as though we were offal. "You cannot touch me I have diplomatic immunity." He smiled like the sly fox he was rumored to be. Too bad for him I'd found a way around his little get out of jail free card. I wish I was the one to break it to him but it was just as good watching my boy Terry do it.

"Not anymore you don't asshole, you fucked with Homeland on this one. Hands behind your back." To say he was displeased would be an understatement.

I kept my cool but with a pissed off look on my face. As an aide to my supposed boss's second hand man I wouldn't have too much to say, I would be too busy worrying about my own ass.

I watched as my team carried out my orders to the letter, couldn't have any fuckups on this one, one wrong move and he'd walk on some trumped up technicality. I had him sewn up nice and tight with all the evidence I'd accumulated in the last couple of months. The only way he could walk is if some asshole played dirty politics at which point I would be going after said asshole.

It took damn near forever to go through the whole ruse of fingerprinting, bail hearings and all the other bullshit that came with a sting. I went through it all in full sight of all the other players so there would be no question that I was who I said I was.

I probably wouldn't be using the same cover ever again but it pays to make this shit look legit in case someone got the bright idea of a payback. I don't trust this KGB fuck no farther than I could spit him, these fuckers are like a six headed snake, you cut one off another springs up to take his place.

The judge had been slipped a fabricated list of all my exploits and since he didn't know that it was all bullshit his reactions were very authentic. I don't trust anyone with my guys, when I'm running an Op it's me and my team that's it. Not even the captain was privy to all that I was doing, he wasn't too happy with it but someone higher up than him, someone that I actually did trust was my handler. He and only he had any kind of say in what I did. So far there haven't been any conflict; that maybe because he knows that the first time there is one I'd walk without a second thought.

I was finally free to slip out of the orange jumpsuit and leave the courthouse hours later. The night was almost over and I was feeling very tired. Weeks of dealing with the dregs of the earth, takes its toll. It was only at the end of an Op that I could find release, this time my release was going to be between the thighs of sweet Jacqueline.

I hurried my pace as thoughts of seeing her face for the first time in three years filled my head. The last picture I'd filched from Mindy's phone files was about three weeks old already.

The two girls had to sneak around to see each other but they'd kept in touch the best they could. I didn't let my sister know what I've been planning until tonight. I almost wanted it to be a surprise, but now that the time was near I wanted her to know I was coming for her.

The anticipation was sweet as fuck, this time tomorrow night I would be cumming inside her sweet tight body.

"Fuck it boss next time you get to do the snort trick, I think I might be slipping I almost inhaled some of that shit this time." Hector ran out behind me complaining like an old woman as usual.

"Suck it up cupcake." He walked next to me to the parking lot where my Harley sat waiting. I hadn't ridden my baby in almost two months. She was probably going to be cranky and give me shit when I hopped on.

"Good job boss, this shit feels good." It did indeed, too bad there will be some other asshole in a day or two either with the same shit or a generic knock off. This shit never ends. At least I'll be laying low for the next little while hopefully they'd give me enough time to get my shit done before they ran wild. Either way I was going to be totally focused on my woman come tomorrow.

Chapter 6

"Summers get in here." The Cap did not sound happy. I wonder what was up his ass this time? There was no love lost between him and I but I liked to keep the peace and since I was going to be gone there was no point in rattling his cage. He'd just use it as an excuse to fuck with my team in my absence and then they'd have to extract my foot from his ass when I came back

"Hey Cap what's up? I can't stay long I need to be on the road in ten." I'd only stopped in to clear off my desk and make sure I didn't leave anything hanging. My guys knew what they needed to do in my absence, that's why they were my guys.

"You took a Russian dignitary into custody without clearing it with me?" He was belligerent and pissed way the fuck off which was his usual attitude when dealing with me. He'd also apparently forgotten to take his meds or some fuck this morning.

My steady glare was all that was

needed to remind him just who the fuck he was talking to, but just in case.

"Uh captain, you seem to be forgetting something." He folded his arms and rocked back and forth on his heels. The potbelly and receding hairline went with the job I guess, too many years of riding a desk and pushing papers.

"I'm still the captain of this precinct and…" I held my hand up out of respect to flow his diarrhea of the mouth.

"My division has nothing to do with your house and you know it. We've been here before you know the drill. You have a problem call up the Supe." I knew he would hate that even more. He resented everything about me, the fact that he thought I was too young to carry the power within the force that I did, the fact that I was a transplant.

He had a shit load of grievances against yours truly and I could give a shit. The Superintendent was my direct boss he's the only one I answered to. Who he answered to I didn't know and didn't care. It was the deal I'd made when I came on board.

I wanted my own team, men and women that held true to the same ideals. People I knew wouldn't shank me in the back for a quick payday. I also wanted full control within reason and that's what I'd gotten.

There had been a lot of rumbling from certain quarters and still were but as long as I kept pulling down the hard jobs they were shitting in the wind. The Supe was my kind of guy, he'd joined the force a hundred years ago it seemed like and he still remembered why he'd done it, and held true. How he got promoted with his clean record is a mystery.

I know damn good and well that the higher you climbed the dirtier the pool, like this fuck standing here in front of me. When I get back, one of the first things I'm going to do is look into his shit.

I've been hearing way too many rumblings of late of evidence in high-ranking cases disappearing, witnesses being gunned down while they were supposed to be under protection.

My division was a separate entity altogether yes, but some of his boys had been slipping through my backdoor at night asking for my expertise. I hated to put them off but I had to until I took care of my shit. That took precedence over everything else. She's been twenty-one for almost a damn year already, but work and commitments had kept me here. Now I was free to go if only this fuck would get his head out his ass already.

"I don't like this one bit." I hope he wasn't expecting me to answer that shit, he knew better, and the fact that he was keeping me from my girl was only burying his ass deeper.

The Supe had asked me to play nice with this asshole so for him I would try but if he fucked with me I'd hand him his ass.

"I'm sure you're well aware by now that I pretty much don't care what you like or dislike. Why don't you write a memo and stick it on that wall over there with all the rest of that shit? I don't work for you, the sooner you get that through your head the sooner we can forego these little chats, now if you're done I've got shit to do and you're fucking with my schedule."

So much for playing nice; but the sight of him standing there looking all pompous when I already knew, and his own men were now coming to believe that he was dirty, was fucking with my head. Men that were supposed to be able to trust him with their lives were afraid to do their jobs because they didn't know if they'd come out alive. I have no respect for his ass and the longer he keeps me in his company the more chance of him finding that shit out, and not in a good way.

After a little more hemming and hawing and fishing for information which he was never going to get from me, I walked out of his office and went to do what I'd come here for in the first place. I needed to be on the road in a few hours. Ever since I'd made that call it's as if my dick had a mind of its own, the fucker's been nagging me on and off for hours. He knew he was going home soon and since we were in the last stretch his patience had worn thin.

"I hear you boy we'll have her soon enough, just a few more hours and we'll get to see her and taste her again."

My guys were sitting around their desks finishing up paperwork from our sting the night before and winding down. Our space was open plan; there was no real hierarchy here since I held such disdain for that shit. My men know who's in charge I didn't need to beat them over the head with that shit. We're a team, this way everyone knows they have my undivided attention and that I'm accessible to each of them at any time.

"Morning boss, you ready to hit the road?" Terry McMann one of my guys walked over to my desk with coffee in hand, more like swaggered. He's the one who'd had the honor of bringing in the Russian last night. I tried to spread shit out, make everyone feel like they were part of what we were doing here. I'm no glory hound, that's for insecure assholes with nothing better to do.

"Morning Terry good job last night, I see you guys got everything squared away all across the board thanks." They beamed like five year olds every last one of them. Who the fuck ever said yelling at and putting down your employees was the most effective way to go needed to be shot.

I don't reward fuck ups, but neither do I berate and I always give praise where it's due. I get more out of my guys and girl than any one man could ask for.

"We've got them tied up nice and tight the boys from DHS were only too happy to swoop them up. Uh Samuels was breathing down our necks when we got here."

"I know we had words, listen all of you, if that asshole puts pressure on any of you you know what to do. Supe will be checking in every once in a while while I'm gone but you call me only if it's an emergency."

They knew some of what I was doing but not all. They knew there was a woman involved because over the years the nosy fucks had wondered why there was never a woman when we hung out with them and theirs.

Once someone had tried a hook up and that shit had went south hard. I'd told the poor blonde to beat it in no uncertain terms. Of course she'd thought I was an asshole, but the idea of even entertaining that thought just felt wrong. There was only one woman I wanted under me and she was a brown-eyed brunette doll with an ass that didn't quit.

"Everything is cleared on my end try to keep your noses clean and do what you know you're supposed to do." That was it in just a few more minutes I'll finally be free for the next ninety days. Now I can look ahead to what came next.

I checked to make sure I had my little surprise with me because when I walked out of this building it was me my bike and the open road. I wasn't taking too much with me because I wasn't planning on staying that long.

I had a place ready for mom and Mindy because there was no way I was going to leave them back there to deal with the backlash. There was just one more thing I had to take care of, my rogue agent, pain in my ass. Thirteen men and only one gave me any trouble.

"Jason you make sure Melissa takes care of herself and don't try any of her shit while I'm gone. No active for her until I get back she can ride a desk and push papers. That ought to keep her little ass out of trouble until she foals." The room erupted in laughter as a half eaten apple came flying at my head.

"You know if you don't make it a rule she's not gonna listen to me Jake." I was busy straightening up the papers and files on my desk and making sure I wasn't leaving anything unfinished.

Leaving for a whole three months was easier said than done though I'd been preparing since I'd put in for the leave with the Supe. The Cap had wanted to get his grubby little hands on my team but I'd nixed that shit in the bud and the Supe had agreed. Yet another reason, for captain asshole to hate my guts. I'd told him point blank I didn't want him anywhere near my men. They played by the rules I set. They did things the way I'd taught them. I didn't need him fucking that shit up in three months.

"Jason for fuck sake she's your woman, she's battling my mustang for size and I don't think she's seen her ankles in two months. How hard can it be to corral her and get her to sit still?" There was a loud scream and a coffee cup was the next thing to come flying across the room.

"You take that back Jake Summers, I'm not as big as your car." I heard her husband cooing at her to calm her down after my well-placed insult. She loves it, six months pregnant and big as a house. I remember when she first broke the news of her pregnancy to the rest of us, the smile on her face, the excitement. She was the first woman I'd ever heard say she was looking forward to getting the belly.

It had given me ideas of planting my own kid. The next three months were going to be devoted entirely to doing just that. "I'll see you guys in a few, try not to destroy the place and if Samuels gets out of hand you have my permission to take him the fuck out. Just don't get caught." With that I was gone.

Chapter 7

Jacqueline

It was easier than I thought to get out of the house, that tree limb that had scared the crap out of me as a child was now my new best friend. I just had to figure out how to get my car down the driveway without making too much noise.

I eased it into drive and with the lights off let it roll slowly backwards down the driveway until I got far enough away from the house to make a U-turn on the lawn and gun it the hell out of there. My heart was racing so fast and hard I felt for sure I was going to collapse.

My hands were actually shaking and my knees felt weak. But then a smile broke out across my face. I'd done it, I'd actually done something I was sure would get me into more trouble than I've been in in a long

long time. I wonder if the fact that both instances had something to do with my Jake was an omen?

That long ago summer when I first felt love… there're no words. He made me feel alive and wanted and sexy and…all the things I'd never felt before in my life. That first night after I'd remembered how my tongue worked we'd talked for hours.

I was breaking curfew but I didn't care, I never wanted to leave his presence. I hadn't missed his reaction when I told him who I was, who my father was. I'd half expected him to give me the brush off just like everyone else did but he hadn't, he'd kept me talking until it was past time to go. I honestly don't remember half of what was said that first night, I was too full of nerves and the look in his eyes kept distracting me.

Everyday that I went to his house under the pretense of tutoring Mindy (who, as far as my parents now believed was a lost cause in the education department) was like an adventure. We worked out a scheme where he would actually help his sister before I even got there and then we'd spend the whole hour or two together.

At first it was just getting to know you stuff. He seemed so attentive, like he really cared about my life. He wanted to know every little detail. The first day he passed his hand through my hair I had a very embarrassing moment, which he of course noticed. He seemed to notice everything about me, which just went straight to my head.

But that day I'd wished he wasn't so observant. With the touch of his fingers against my scalp my skin had heated, I'd become flushed and the seat of my panties was a whole lot wetter than they had been. I don't think he would've noticed all of that though if I hadn't moaned out loud and clenched my thighs together. Then again it had worked out for the best because that was the first time he'd kissed me.

He'd looked right into my eyes then and stolen my heart with one touch of his lips against mine. I almost ate the poor man's face off so green was I. It was the first time anyone had ever kissed me and boy was I not prepared. He did everything just right, from the way he held my head in his hands, the slow way he moved in while keeping eye contact and then that first tentative brush of lips. He'd nibbled on my bottom lip once, twice, three times, and then he'd taken my tongue into his mouth and suckled. After that my panties were pretty much useless.

"Do you ever see yourself living anywhere else but here sweet Jacqueline?" I love it when he calls me that, love the way he touches me when he says it. We were in his family's living room. The house was small but neat and full of little happy mementos.

His mom made her own curtains of all things and crocheted little throw things for the chairs and stuff. Nothing at all like the professionally decorated mausoleum I'd grown up in.

"I don't know I've never really given it much thought before." How was I supposed to spend the rest of my life with him if I couldn't remember how to breathe in his presence? He had this intense way of looking into my eyes when we talked, as if all his attention was solely focused on me and me alone. When I'm with him I don't feel like the social misfit or the plain Jane I'd always believed myself to be.

"One day I'm going to steal you away from here." He said it jokingly but all I could think was 'yes please and thank you.' "When?" Crap I hadn't meant to say that out loud. Now he'll think I'm a needy little girl too green to know when a boy was just sweet-talking her. "Soon I promise." Those words had warmed my heart. I'd never doubted for one second that he'd meant them.

We spent the whole summer kissing on that couch or sometimes when I was feeling brave enough, while lying across his bed in his old room. The first time he lifted my shirt I almost died.

"No baby don't tense up I'm not going to hurt you just let me look at you." He'd studied me for the longest time and then his nostrils had flared and...

"I'm sorry, I lied." He growled those words just before he lowered his head and took my nipple into his mouth. My womb was no longer speaking, she was screeching at the top of her lungs for me to get on with it. I think this is what they mean by self-combusting, at least it should be.

Every surface of my skin felt like it was on fire, my breathing was shot and I don't think I remembered how to hold a thought. He chewed on my nipple and I'm almost ashamed to say I couldn't hold back the unladylike sounds that escaped me. My hand of its own accord came up to hold his head in place and when he shifted his thigh between mine...well, lets just say I rode that horse for all he was worth.

"Fuck we have to stop." What why who says? Those were my confused rambling thoughts as I fought to hold onto my sanity. I tried to get his leg back to where it had been a minute ago but he held me off. "I can't take you with my little sister in the other room babe. When I take you it might get loud…"

"I don't care Jake please…" I tried again, I don't know quite what I was begging for but I knew I needed something. This ache he'd started inside of me wasn't going away and he needed to put a stop to it right damn now.

I've never felt that aggressive and almost violent before in my life, it was as though someone else had taken over my body. I ached so bad tears formed in my eyes. "Shh, shh, come 'ere baby it's okay."

"It hurts." He looked down at me then and back at the door. "You're killing me here you know that?"

I didn't answer, couldn't. Just looked at him with what must've been the most pitiful sight he'd ever seen because he'd sat up on the side of the bed and removed his shirt. Then he'd started on me and oh my.

My panties were stripped down my thighs and my legs spread over his shoulders. He'd looked at me down there until I turned red and then he'd done what I at first thought was the oddest thing but then learned was the most amazing thing on earth.

He licked me. Right there on my kitty, his tongue felt like nothing I'd ever felt before, rough and hard and smooth and shit I couldn't tell. It just felt too good to describe.

I tried picking up my head to look down at him, but the bones in my neck were no longer working. And when he lifted me into his mouth and sunk his tongue deep inside me I came in his mouth...hard. So much for being quiet.

"Shh baby." He lifted his hand to cover my mouth and I thought biting him sounded like the best idea, so I did. And he thrust that tongue harder and faster and my body moved in ways I never taught it to. He pulled his tongue out and I came close to killing another human being for the first time in my life.

But then he did something wonderful with that tongue, he licked my clit, and two long hard fingers sunk into my kitty and she yowled.

"Jake what's happening?" Leave it to me to die just when I'd found paradise because that's what it felt like, like I was going to draw my last breath any minute now.

"Just go with it baby." Easy for him to say; he kept up that licking and fingering and growling into my flesh. When I came again he climbed up my body and covered it with his and I tasted myself on his tongue for the first time while he pressed his hardness between my thighs.

That was the beginning of the best summer of my life. After that I was like a bee drawn to honey, every moment we were alone together I wanted more and that's how we'd ended up in the backseat of his car that night.

We'd gone out of town for the first time ever that night, I was too afraid to be seen anywhere in our town with him because I knew daddy would put an end to us and I couldn't have that.

Jake seemed to understand and didn't argue about it. He'd taken me to a movie and dinner. We'd sat next to each other in a secluded booth and held hands and stole kisses while we shared our food. It was the most freeing experience of my life. By then we had been making out almost everyday for two whole months and I thought I was pretty worldly.

He'd taught me things about myself that I could never forget. I could never go back to being that girl that I'd been before and I wished more than anything that I could have him for always. Though he'd never pressured me I knew it couldn't be easy for him to hold back all this time.

He'd taught me how to take him into my mouth and please him, that was my new favorite thing and I loved it when he teased me about it. As soon as we were alone together my knees hit the floor. I loved that best until he taught me how to suck his cock while he ate my pussy.

Jake said little girls had kitties and women had pussies, and even though the word made me blush I was getting use to saying it and hearing him he tell me how sweet mine was.

I can't take all the blame for that night because Jake had started it. During dessert he'd worked his hand up under my dress and fingered me right there in the restaurant while the waiter went back and forth. It was a test to see if I could be quiet. I damn near bit a whole in my lip trying to keep my animalistic grunts and groans at bay.

When we'd left I'd moaned and groaned until he took me out to the football field. I thought it would be safe there, school was out and no one ever really hung around out there as far as I knew. It was a chance for us to be alone together.

I didn't dare suggest a hotel room because that would've been far too brazen so this was the next best thing.

"I don't think this is such a good idea baby." He turned to me after parking the car. The night was warm and bright and the stars blanketed the sky, it was a perfect night for lovers, just like all those romance novels I used to sneak and read.

"And why not?" He looked at me and then back at the seat behind us. "Because I have a hard enough time keeping my cock out of you when there're people around that's why." He has such a way with words my Jake does.

"Don't be silly we'll be fine, I trust you." My ass, I've been reading, and I know more than enough to know just what it was I wanted. Pretty soon he'd be leaving again, we'd talked about it.

His idea was that we wait until I finished school, hah later for that. I wanted to know what it felt like to have more than his tongue or his fingers inside me. And though the feel of his hardness in my mouth was a bit intimidating I couldn't wait to feel it plunging in and out of me. He was playing it safe for my sake I guess but I knew just how to get him where I needed.

I played the coy virgin, which in all essence I was, but he had no idea what I had in store for him. I started off by nibbling on his neck while running my hand across his chest. He likes it when I tease his ears with my tongue so that was next on my agenda.

"Sweetheart you better stop." Yeah right. I turned up the heat by letting my hand drop innocently into his lap and teasing his cock (another new word that now trips off my tongue with ease). I knew I had him when his hands fisted in my hair and he took my mouth hungrily.

Before I knew it we were in the backseat and my dress was up around my waist. His mouth was on my pussy while his fingers dug into the flesh of my ass and I was cumming again. I pulled his head harder into me as he sucked on me like I was his last meal.

Jake

Shit she played me. My sweet innocent girl had used my body against me and she used everything I'd taught her to do it. I never wanted this for her; I wanted her first time to be special. Maybe on our wedding night even, but she had decided and I was coming to learn that there was nothing I would deny her.

She was so fucking sweet, and shy. But all that shyness melted away when we were together like this. I never get enough of her taste in my mouth, the more I ate her sweet pussy the more I wanted. My cock was hard and hurting but that was nothing new, every time she left me feeling like this. I've fucked her mouth more than I've pissed the whole summer and still it wasn't enough. Still I'd been willing to wait, to do things right. She pulled on my hair and begged me to take her. "Please Jake don't make me beg."

"Baby…" I tried one last time for propriety's sake. It wasn't right to fuck the future mother of my children in the backseat of a second hand car.

"If you don't do it Jake Summers then someone else will." That shit made me see red. I had my hand around her throat and the other covering her pussy before she drew her next breath.

"Don't ever say that shit to me again, you ever even think of fucking someone else I'll kill you." She smiled up at me the little sneak and wiggled her ass pressing her hot cunt into me.

"Well then…get on with it." I groaned in defeat even as I undid my pants. I'd had my fingers and tongue inside her enough to know that she was small. There was no way she was going to be able to take all of me especially not in the cramped space we were in.

I took my time after my cock was free, rubbing the head back and forth over her clit and down to her opening. She mewled in that sweet way that makes my cock weep.

"Look at me." She looked into my eyes as I eased part of my length into her. I tested her body little by little until I felt the barrier. Pulling back almost all the way I plunged forward hard and fast covering her mouth with mine to catch the scream I knew was coming.

When her body had adjusted and my head no longer felt like it would explode I started moving inside her. Short easy strokes at first until she gripped me with her hot cunt and I couldn't help but move faster.

I wanted to consume her; the need for her was so strong it was almost frightening. I pulled my strokes not willing to hurt her even as my body begged me to fuck. She raised her legs and dug her nails into my ass trying to get more of me inside her, so I gave her another inch or so but still not all. Whether she knew it or not that would hurt her and I wanted this night to be remembered only for its pleasure.

"Fuck baby your pussy's so tight." She was moving as best she could in the confined space, rubbing her clit against me for added relief. I could see her reaching for orgasm so I used my thumb to tease her clit while deep stroking her pussy.

I was close, so fucking close and we'd only just started, months of pent up lust was in play. All those times I'd eaten her pussy and nothing else were coming back to bite me in the ass, I needed to flood her with my cum but I needed even more to make her scream.

"Cum for me sweet Jacqueline." I teased the entrance to her ass with my finger without going in. I hadn't introduced her to anal play as yet, that wasn't big on my list but the added stimulation could only bring her off faster. That coupled with whispered words of love did the trick.

She tightened around my cock and bit my tongue as she flooded my cock with pussy juice. I went off like a shot until I remembered almost too late to pull out. I sprayed her lower stomach and pussy hair with cum as I stroked the last bit of my seed out of the end of my cock.

Chapter 8

Jacqueline

Mindy was at the designated spot waiting for me. I pulled up next her car and rolled down my windows. "Just follow me Jackie, this is gonna be so much fun." She was way too excited about this if you ask me. Here I was not sure what my life would hold come morning, because yes the last ten minutes alone in my car I've had time to think about this and…freaking shit I was a goner.

I hadn't thought of how I was getting back into the house without detection, hadn't thought of anything at all except escaping.

I followed her cute little roadster that I'm sure her brother had bought for her when she turned twenty-one a few months after me. I had been green with envy and hurt at the time but I understood. He couldn't contact me in anyway because daddy had threatened his family. It made me wonder how Mindy was so brave to thwart his position and try to be my friend anyway.

Some days I was so mad at Jake for not coming back, especially the night of my twenty first birthday. I'd been so sure he'd be there to get me but no. Instead I'd spent it with daddy and mom at a quiet dinner in a stuffy restaurant. I couldn't even mourn his absence in peace because as soon as daddy saw me looking anything but upbeat he went on the warpath. That night has been used as an anvil over my head for three damn years.

We pulled into the packed parking lot of the club Mindy has been raving about since she became old enough to drink. She'd let it slip once that Jake had laid down the law about her drinking and partying before she was old enough, and she'd held true to her promise not to.

Those two were so close it was amazing to me that he hadn't returned at least to see her and his mom. Though I knew they'd gone to visit him more than once but because of my stupid rule not to talk about him I hadn't heard any of the details.

I wasn't sure about this place, I've never stepped foot inside of one and this one looked a bit crowded if the number of cars and trucks were anything to go by.

"Come on don't chicken out on me now. You're not going to believe it, let's go inside and get you your first cocktail and then we'll talk." She was jumpier than a bullfrog in a marsh.

"What's with you anyway? You and Dylan getting hitched or something?" She grinned and hugged my arm closer to her as she dragged me towards mayhem.

Inside it was loud and crowded and dark. There were people everywhere and I don't know how anyone could see where they were going because there was no space.

The music thumped so hard I felt it in my chest, and we had to press through bodies to get to the bar. As the seconds went by I felt...free. I actually felt alive in this place for the first time since Jake had left me.

There was a sense of excitement in the air, maybe Mindy's was rubbing off on me. She had to yell our orders at the blonde giant behind the bar who looked like he ate small children and assorted animals for breakfast. I tried to avoid the leering looks from some of the patrons as they checked out my ass. Maybe this wasn't such a good idea after all. I have no idea what to do if one of them asked me to dance.

"What did you get me?" She gave me something that looked like coffee with milk in a glass with ice. I sniffed it to make sure and the scent of alcohol hit my nose. "A screaming orgasm." My mouth almost hit the floor even as my cheeks reddened. I can't believe she'd ordered such a thing. "Is that really the name of a drink?" She rolled her eyes and nodded as she took a sip if her matching beverage.

"It's so good you should taste yours." I took a tentative sip and she was right, it was good. Sweet and yummy, my first taste of the forbidden juice. She was back to dragging me off again and looking around as if searching for someone.

There was enough energy jumping off of her to light up the skyline. Probably Dylan, she always acts like that when he's around. We found a corner that was less crowded and stood back to watch the revelers.

"So what did you want to tell me?" I had to shout to be heard above the music. She was still busy looking around and I wondered how she expected to find anyone in this.

"In a minute." She got to her toes and started looking over shoulders. I decided to ignore her crazy and enjoy my drink. I could get used to this. She suddenly screamed like someone was killing her and grabbed onto me while jumping up and down.

I heard a voice say, 'there she is' one second before I was crushed up against a hard chest and lips covered mine. I know that mouth, sweet merciful heavens…everything inside me went south and I held on tight after dropping my forgotten drink on the floor. It was a while before my lips were freed and I looked up into the most beautiful face I'd ever seen.

"Jake?" My voice was barely above a whisper, it's all I could muster right now, but somehow he heard me.

"It's me baby." He grabbed a fistful of my hair and pulled my head back, staring down at me for the longest while. And then a smile broke out across his gorgeous face.

Chapter 9

Jacqueline

He pulled me in close and hugged me so tight. My heart beat hard against my ribs and my knees turned to liquid. And though it felt like my bones were being crushed to powder, it was the sweetest, most precious hug in the world.

No one had ever felt the way I did right now, they couldn't. There's no way another human being had ever felt this intense love, it was not to be borne. I buried my nose in his chest inhaling his scent. He was a wild mix of leather, his own natural scent and something spicy that all blended together to make the most potent ovary stimulating concoction.

My Jake was here, he was really here; I returned his hug the best I could. The crowded room had ceased to exist the moment he pulled me into his arms, there was only the two of us and nothing else mattered, nothing.

Above the thump, thump, thump, of my heart I felt his, and then it happened, that's when I did it. The one thing I'd always promised myself I would never do if and when we met again. I cried like a newborn babe.

Clutching at him I let the past three years of fear and frustration and loneliness pour forth. He hugged me around the shoulders with one arm while running the other up and down my back soothingly while whispering softly in my ear.

"I'm taking her out of here Mindy, you good?" I lifted my head and looked back at the forgotten Mindy who had her hands clasped in front of her mouth as if in prayer as tears streamed down her face. She nodded yes to her brother just as Dylan appeared at her side and put his arms around her. "I've got her Jake you guys go on."

Jake released me long enough to grab my hand and pull us through the crowd.

Who he didn't push out of the way automatically parted to let us through. Did I forget to mention that Jake is a giant? Okay that's a bit of an exaggeration but he is at least six four. I'm sure the leather jacket over the tank with the tattoos on his neck and some of the ones on his chest peeping through added to the visage of a badass.

People just automatically got out of the way and pretty soon we were in the cool night air. His grip on my hand was tight and sure and gave me strength. I don't know what was coming next but I knew this time I was going to fight.

"Let's go baby we'll take my bike and come back for your car later." He pulled me over to this monstrosity of black and chrome. I'm not an expert but I do believe it's what people in the know might call a sweet ride.

Jake

"Where're we going?" I led her over to my bike and helped her put on the custom made helmet I'd brought for her. "You'll see." I helped her on behind me and we peeled out of the parking lot heading even farther away from our hometown.

Ten minutes later we were checking into the only hotel this place had which I'd booked way in advance. No words were spoken as I led her up the stairs to the room on the second floor and flung the door open.

"We have to be somewhere in an hour but I can't wait to have you...fuck." I pulled her to me again and attacked her sweet mouth.

She tasted better than my fading memory recalled. It had been too long. I pushed her down on the bed and tackled the buckle of her belt before tearing at her jeans to get them off. I got them down but her boots thwarted me as her jeans got caught up.

Calm down Jake shit. I had to take a deep breath before I could go on. Taking my time though it was killing me I lifted first one foot then the other so I could pull her boots off. With that done I pulled her pants off the rest of the way.

I didn't allow myself to look just yet. I went after the top next. I wanted to rip it off of her but she wouldn't have anything to wear out of here if I did that. Tomorrow we'll have a discussion as to why she wasn't allowed to wear that shit ever again, too much of what's mine on display there.

"Hurry Jake…" She attacked my jacket, pushing it down off my shoulders before she latched onto my neck with her teeth. She remembered and so did my dick.

I was trying to block him out because his impatient ass would only hurt her if I gave into his needs before making sure she was ready. I helped her shed the rest of my clothes after she was naked.

"Jake what's that?" I looked down at where she was pointing at my cock. "What my cock piercing?" I looked up in time to see the look of hurt and jealousy flash across her face.

"No baby it's not what you're thinking. I got this when I was at a very low point, I figured the pain from having this done would save me from doing something very stupid." She looked up at me with her innocent eyes and my heart turned over in my chest.

"Something like what?" I took her cheek in my hand as our eyes held, so precious, so fucking unbelievably sweet.

"Like fucking someone else. I didn't want to do that, so when my need for you got to be too much and I was ready to climb the fucking walls I went and let some asshole do this to my dick. It worked too, shit took weeks to heal, by then I was used to it, I kinda like it, you will too I promise."

She knelt in the middle of the bed and reached for me trying to take me into her mouth. "Oh no baby if you suck on me right now I'll go off like a shot, I haven't even stroked my cock in three months in anticipation of this moment, no way I'm spilling in your mouth." She pouted her sweet pout, which drew me to her mouth for another kiss before she pulled away.

"So you didn't…you know…with anyone else?" Cool, I guess we needed to have this little convo first though my dick was leaking pre cum like a son of a bitch.

"Babe didn't you hear anything I said to you that night?" She bit her lip and lowered her head. "I know Jake but that was a long time ago and…" I lifted her chin again so I could see into her eyes.

"That's just time baby, time doesn't change love, love is forever." She flew into my arms and wrapped her arms and legs around me.

"I love you so much Jake." She was back to crying and peppering my face with kisses. "Fuck baby I've waited so long to hear you say that, say it again." She repeated it over and over as I laid her back on the bed and spread her open for my eyes to feast. "Stand up babe I want to see that ass."

Jacqueline

I stood at the side of the bed as he inspected me, my body shaking in need. He slapped one cheek and bit the other making me squeal in surprise.

"Jake what're you doing?" I laughed down at him as he continued to cover my ass with little love nips.

"Marking you." His hand cupped my pussy and his fingers teased with feather light touches. There was a heat there and I wasn't sure if it was from me, or him but it felt amazing.

"Bend over baby." He had me lean over the bed while he moved around behind me and…sweet mercy he was licking me from behind. I gripped the sheets as he held my hips steady for the onslaught of his tongue.

"Oh…Jake feels so good." He moved his head form side to side as he pushed his tongue deeper inside me. I couldn't help it, I might smother the poor man with my need but I pushed back against his tongue begging for more.

"I want to fuck you so bad from behind baby but not this time. This time I want you beneath me."

He laid me across the bed himself, which was good because I'd lost all movement in my limbs; I was a limp mess. I noticed for the first time the diamond stud he now sported in his left ear.

As if he needed to add anything more to his devastatingly handsome self. It was hot and sexy and made me want to do all manner of lascivious things to him.

He ran the piercing in his cock over my tummy making me tremble before he and it went after my clit. Shock waves ran through my body at the feel of the cold metal against my warm flesh. Then he pressed down and in and I felt that remembered fullness.

"Hold on sweetheart." I had no time to

contemplate his meaning before I was being torn in two. My loud screech could be heard I'm sure by the other guests it was that loud. The pleasure pain was unlike anything I'd ever known. There was a burning and a heat and yet a need that was too strong for me to comprehend.

Jake

"Unghh." There was a touch of pain in her voice that brought me up short.

"What? Am I hurting you?" I looked down at her body. Her legs were opened around my hips, her body laid bare for my eyes, hands and mouth to feast on.

"Just a little, I don't remember you being this...big." She blushed prettily as she tried to hide her face in the pillow beneath her head.

"Babe when I took your cherry I only used about seven of my ten inches." I pulled back a little to ease her discomfort.

"Oh..." She looked at me almost in wonder as I slid back in. I cautioned myself to go easy even though my cock was like a bull at the rodeo gate. One sniff of her and he was ready to break out, like me he knew her, knew who she was, and what she meant to us.

"I'll go easy baby just lift your leg a little. Good girl." I kept her leg over my bent arm as I once again stroked in and out of her sweet pussy. That tight grip I remembered, that had been the cause of many a sleepless night was still there only better. I felt the most intense rush of possession as her body gave in to me.

"Mine..." She arched her back and cried out at my loud growl, this time in pleasure. I felt her give way to me inside, felt her body stretch to accept my length and I let go.

Jacqueline

Something was forming inside of me. It was hard and sweet and hot and the pleasure pain of it was too much to put into words. I thought I would die from it as he pounded away inside me, nothing had ever felt this good. And then the most amazing thing happened.

That ball had been forming unfurled and I felt a burst of lust and love so strong I lost sight for just that one moment in time. I clung to him biting into his neck the way I know he likes as I felt the thumping of his cock inside my tummy. From his loud growl and 'fuck, fuck, fuck' I knew he was cumming. It went on for a long time before his body finally fell onto mine.

Chapter 10

Jake

When I could finally feel my ass again I checked my watch. "We've got fifteen minutes to get cleaned up and be somewhere." I eased my still semi hard cock out of her. I'd like nothing better than to stay here buried balls deep inside her for the rest of the night but this was too important to put off.

"Where're we going again?" She moved kind of gingerly as she crawled off the bed. I'm going to have to be more careful with her, kinda ease her into taking my whole length I guess.

"There's a judge waiting to marry us, I would ask if you were okay with that but you don't have a choice." She flew at me again and hugged the shit out of my neck. "Really Jake, really?" I hugged her and carried her to the bathroom for a quick cleanup.

I'm sure this wasn't her idea of the perfect wedding, to be dressed in jeans and me in leathers, but the deed was more important than the party. I figure somewhere in the next fifty or sixty years she could have the wedding of her dreams, right now I'm more interested in the marriage side of the deal. That piece of paper that said she belongs to me. As long as I have that under my belt I can take on all comers.

I let her wash my cock since she seemed so fascinated by the barbell under the crown but when she tried to climb me to force me inside her I held her off.

"I'm not fucking you with soap on my dick baby that can't be good for your little pussy and besides we don't have time." She gave me her sweet pout again and I rinsed us both off and took her out of the shower while she kept running her hands all over me. That shit felt good.

I helped her back into her clothes because she was too busy teasing my ass to distraction and then I got my shit back on, grabbed her hand and went down to checkout.

We were at the judge's place on time and it took us less than ten minutes for her to become solely and completely mine. Nothing in my life ever felt this fucking fulfilling, not when I graduated top of my class in college, not when I was given rule of my own division, nothing. This moment was the catalyst for what would be my most important undertaking on the earth.

My woman, I was now responsible completely for her heart, her joys and her sorrows. Hopefully there won't be too much of the latter. "Let's go baby I have to take you to see mom." I had to go introduce my wife to her new mother in law. My wife, fuck that felt good, almost as good as her arm around my waist as we walked back outside.

The next few days were going to be a flurry of movement; I had no intentions on spending anymore time in this hellhole than was absolutely necessary.

We got back on my bike and headed back the way we came. Mom didn't even know I was here only Mindy knew, she'd been my partner in crime in this little scheme I had going.

I'd put a lot on her over the years. In the beginning when she'd told me that my girl didn't want to hear about me because it was too hard I'd wanted nothing more than to come back here and take her. But I'd bided my time and stuck to my long term plans hoping all the while that she could wait for me. Now she was finally mine and nothing was going to take her away from me ever again.

We were two minutes into the town limits when I heard the sirens. Fuck what now? I pulled over and helped her off. "No matter what happens stay here, do not move." The cruiser pulled in behind us and stopped and out stepped a deputy. He looked vaguely familiar but I couldn't quite place him until he opened his mouth.

"I guess you don't learn so good do

you boy? Come on Jackie get in the car."
Had he looked at her with lust in his eyes the
last time we'd met? I can't remember, I'd
been too focused on her then but I saw it
now.

I remember the last time I'd seen him.
It was the night he'd shone a flashlight into
the backseat of my car. I remember he'd put
his hands on her like he had every right.
How he'd made her get into the front of his
cruiser.

She'd begged me not to fight that
night and even though I'd wanted to, back
then I'd been more about using my brain
instead of brawn. I knew I wouldn't gain
anything by going up against them. I was
fresh out of college and only a few months
into my new career.

Tonight though I didn't give a fuck, I
picked that fucker up and threw him across
the street. Jacqueline called out to me but I
stopped her with a raised hand. "Don't move
remember?" She'd started to walk towards
me.

I walked over to him and stood over

his dazed form. He started mouthing off about what he was going to do to me but I had just the thing to shut him up. Even though this was a two-bit town in the middle of nowhere I'm sure they'd got the memo. I made sure of it.

Jacqueline

Oh no not again, I was too scared to even move, I've never seen anyone get thrown that far except on TV. I was sure this was not going to turn out good. Jake pulled something from under his shirt. I couldn't see what it was because it was dark. I know it wasn't a gun because it was hanging from a chain around his neck, but whatever it was it had Deputy Culver receding in fear.

"You ever come near her again it'll be that last fucking thing you ever do. Now get the fuck gone." Deputy Culver jumped to his feet and ran to his car while Jake walked cool as a cucumber back to me.

"You know he's only going to run to daddy Jake." And what do you expect him to do Jackie, kill him? Yes, yes I do. Kill the little sneak and bury his ass out here in the woods. Great now you want your new husband to commit murder.

"Don't worry about that I have to face him sometime." And why did it seem like he was just chomping at the bit for that one?

We reached mom's house and I could see that she was still worrying when we got off the bike.

"Baby you have nothing to worry about. That ring on your finger means that I fight all your battles from now on okay." Damn I could look at her face all day she has this way of looking at me as though I'm the answer to her every prayer.

Taking her hand I led her into the house. "Mom where are you?" I heard a scream and then she came running from her room in the back. She came up short when she saw Jacqueline's hand clasped in mine but then she caught herself and came forward to hug me.

"You bad boy why didn't you let me know you were coming?" I pushed her shoulders back so I could look down at her.

"I wanted it to be a surprise and so is this. Mom meet your new daughter in law." She was shocked to say the least and looked back and forth between us.

"You mean you two…" I lifted my wife's hand with the ring and showed her. "Oh Jake." She started wringing her hands and it pissed me the fuck off that even my own mother was still afraid of that sanctimonious asshole.

"Don't worry mom everything's going to be fine." I hugged her again to reassure her and then led them both into the house. Jacqueline was a little shy and unsure of herself but I knew she would overcome that soon enough. I was going to have a hell of a time on my hands undoing all the shit her fuck of a sperm donor had done.

Mindy showed up ten minutes later and the women got to yakking about the ring and the wedding and I had to hear a lecture from my mother about weddings and what they mean to young girls and shit.

Not long after I heard the sound of the engine that I'd been expecting pulling up outside. They all got quiet and stared towards the door. I'm sure the events of three years ago were uppermost on all their minds. "I've got it." I walked purposefully towards the door and opened it to a pissed off Gary Willoughby.

"There something I can do for you?" Puffed up asshole was still trying to look down his nose at me even though I was a good six inches taller.

"I understand that my daughter's in there I've come to take her home." I folded my arms and looked down at him blocking his way.

"She's not going anywhere with you, anything else?" He got huffy and stepped towards me, oh please do; just once throw the first punch. "Now see here, now apparently you didn't hear me last time…"

"I have no interest in anything you have to say now if that's all I suggest you get the fuck gone." I knew that wouldn't work I was banking on it, that's why I didn't close the door when I turned and walked away. He followed me inside and started his shit right away.

"Mom go into your room, close the door and turn the TV up as loud as it would go." She was back to wringing her hands and looking close to tears.

"Son I don't…" I went to her and turned her around all the while making sure to keep my body between Jacqueline and the asshole. She left reluctantly but when I turned to Mindy she just outright told me she wasn't budging.

"I'm not going anywhere." She put on her stubborn ass face and I decided to choose my battles. I waited until I heard the TV in mom's room blaring before turning back to the scene unfolding behind me. The asshole was ripping into my wife and I was two minutes away from tearing him a new one, now with mom gone I could deal with his stupid ass.

Jacqueline

"You don't fucking talk to her like that again."

"Let's go Jacqueline I won't tell you again."

"She's not going anywhere with you old man and before you even think of trying anything know that I'm not the same kid you ran off the last time. So you and your pals better think twice before you fuck with what's mine."

"You're nothing but a poor whelp from the wrong side of the tracks, if you think I would let my daughter sully herself with the likes of you you've got another think coming."

Daddy reached out to grab me but Jake was faster. He pushed me behind his back and blocked my dad's view. I was never so scared in my life. It was happening all over again. When will it end? I wanted so badly to believe Jake when he said everything was going to be okay but I know daddy. He's mean and spiteful and he can hold a grudge, I should know I've been at the receiving end of one for three years.

"Jacqueline I said get your ass over here now."

"Jake..." I cried out when he reached for daddy, holding him by his neck.

"You talk to her like that again it'll be the last time you do it with a full head of teeth. Now just so you know old man the only reason I haven't laid your ass out already is out of respect for her but you keep disrespecting her and all bets are off."

"You don't scare me, I've got friends… "

"Yes I remember all about your friends but this time I'm not alone. This time I've got the law on my side."

"The law, what law? I own the law around here boy." Jake pulled that thing from beneath his shirt again and I saw that it was some sort of shield. It looked like a cop's but there was something else written on it that I couldn't make out.

I saw the fire in daddy's eyes, I know him so well he was livid. He wanted to pummel Jake if the closed fists and clenched teeth were any indication but at least he had the good sense not to try.

"I don't care about your badge she's my daughter and she's coming home with me."

"She's old enough to make her own decisions, only this one I've already made for her."

"You've lost your mind, I'll bury you if you don't stay out of my way."

"Go ahead old man I'd like to see you try."

"This is still my town, all I have to do is tell the sheriff what you've done here… "

"Oh yeah and what's that?"

"You've kidnapped her of course, holding her against her will." Daddy started to smile after making that vile threat. That sickening smile he always wore right before he pounced, and I felt bile rise in the pit of my gut. Why was I always so weak? Why couldn't I stand up to him?

"You'd have a hard time proving that one since she can always tell them she's here of her own free will."

"She'll tell them what I say won't you little girl?" He tried looking around Jake at me but Jake shifted his body shielding me from the venom in daddy's eyes. "I'll disown her otherwise."

"Go ahead, disown her, she doesn't need you or your money." He grinned at Jake like the cat that ate the canary.

"You think she'd walk away from millions for you? A nobody with a dead end job? How much do you make a year? Thirty, forty thousand? With what she stands to inherit she could buy and sell you ten times over. Or is that what you've been after all along? Fancy living up on the hill? You see Jacqueline he's just been using you."

"Hey asshole you address me, you have nothing more to say to her." I guess Jake felt my fear in the death grip I suddenly had on the back of his jeans.

"She's my daughter... "

"Yeah? Well she's my wife." I peaked around Jake long enough to see daddy take a step back. His face had gone completely red and he was sweating. Never a good sign, he was about to blow. My knees started to shake and I moaned out loud. This was my biggest fear come true.

"Is this true?" Daddy tried addressing me again but once more Jake stopped him.

"Are you fucking death? I said don't fucking talk to her. You've said all the fuck you have to say to her now you can leave or I'll help your ass leave."

Daddy was mad for sure, his eyes were about to pop and so was that vein in his neck, the one that always jumped right before he attacked. I wanted to close my eyes against what was coming next but something extraordinary happened just then.

Daddy didn't move quite fast enough to suit Jake and so he stepped forward crowding him. And daddy shook; he actually looked around as if seeking escape. I felt the first kernel of hope unfurl at the sight.

To see daddy all but cowering before someone else, the tyrant who had ruled over everyone and everything in my life with an iron fist was actually afraid. Jake leaned in and whispered something in his ear that had him looking pretty close to what Deputy Culver had looked like earlier.

"Get… the fuck… gone." Jake leaned in close and growled those words at daddy and he actually turned and left, unbelievable. Was it over? It couldn't be over.

"Come here baby." Jake kept his eyes on the door as he reached back to pull me around. I plastered myself to his chest and finally gave in to the shakes.

"It's okay precious girl I've got you." Mindy came up behind me and wrapped her arms around both of us and Jake extended his hug to hold her too. I felt safely cocooned between my two stalwart warriors.

Chapter 11

Jake

Mom snuck out of her room a few minutes later. "Is he gone?" I released the girls and went to her drawing her still shaking form into my arms.

"He's gone mom. You don't have to be afraid because you're not staying here. When I leave here I'm taking you with me." She looked up at me about to argue but I didn't give her a chance.

"You did what I asked you to?" I spoke to Mindy over her head. "Yeah the movers will be here tomorrow." Mom looked back and forth between us.

"Movers?" I knew she was going to have a hard time leaving, this is where she'd spent her life with dad but there was no way

I was leaving her here alone. And since I had no intentions on coming back here again this was the only option.

"Yeah I had Mindy call a moving company to come get your stuff. I know I should've talked it over with you first mom but you're just too stubborn when it comes to this place. You know you can't stay here and you damn sure can't work for that…for Willoughby again."

Mindy decided to choose that moment to show her little hellion side. "Oh mom you should've seen it, Jake handed him his ass. No hard feelings Jackie, but your dad is a dick. Jake is the champ woot." She walked around the room like Rocky until mom curtailed her celebration.

"Mindy Elizabeth Summers you watch you mouth, whatever he may be he's still the father of your new sister in law and no matter how awful a person may be their children still loves them." Mindy looked at Jacqueline who was once again clinging to my neck.

"Sorry Jackie I wasn't thinking, don't

mind me and my big mouth." I hugged her tighter wishing only to be alone with her so I could love her out of her misery but there was still a lot to be done.

"Now mom I don't want you to worry I've got it all worked out, I've got a place for you and Mindy already. The movers will just be taking grandma's furniture and your clothes and stuff like that, everything else has already been taken care of."

I tried to let go of my wife but she wasn't having it so I held on as I walked us both to the couch in the living room. "I don't know son, you just got married and everything you need your space." I sat Jacqueline down on the couch and turned to my mother and sister.

"Come over here and sit down both of you." I made room on the couch for mom on the other side of me, and Mindy sat in the side chair.

"I bought a house. It's a nice place in a nice area, mom you can finally retire, you're fifty years old but you've been working since the age of thirteen that's more than enough. Now I've got pictures of the house if you want to see it but you're going." I asked Mindy to get her laptop so that I could cue up the virtual tour videos I'd had made of the new house.

"It's one of those mother daughter type things, mom you'll have your side and we'll have ours. I was thinking Mindy could take the condo if she can prove that she's responsible enough to be on her own."

They looked at the pictures and the cooing started. The three of them deserted me and headed for the table where they could all see together. "Geez big brother how much money do you make anyway this place is huge?" My sister has no tack.

"Enough." They were busy for the next hour or so looking at rooms and planning decoration parties and what the fuck ever, I was just happy that they were happy. Jacqueline came and sat beside me with her head on my shoulder. "It's okay baby we'll be fine." She got closer and sniffled into my neck.

"I'm not gonna get to say bye to

mom." I kissed her hair and hugged her close, if she wanted to see her mom no force on earth was going to stop her, not as long as there was breath in my body.

"You want to see her you'll see her tomorrow before we leave." She picked up her head and looked at me like I was nuts. "He won't…"

"I told you before let me worry about your old man I've got this."

"So Jake can I come work for you? It looks to be a cushy job." Mindy grinned over at me, always starting trouble. "No you can't it's not for you."

"I bet you'd let Jackie do it."

"No I wouldn't, no disrespect baby but that shit is not for you. I have one female on my team and she's well, she's not your average female. She came from a place of violence so she knows how to handle that shit. You on the other hand are soft and sweet. Besides you've had enough hardships in your life as it is you don't need that shit."

It was much later when everyone was finally ready to go to bed. I was hard as a pike, had been for the past few hours. But if I took her here the whole damn house would know. I fixed that little issue by dragging the mattress onto the floor when she made it known that she wanted her man to fuck her.

"You need me to stuff something in your mouth to keep your little ass quiet?" She sat up on the bed and reached for my swinging dick.

"Yes, this." She had me in her mouth before I could even take my next breath. She played with my cock piercing running her tongue and teeth around the little balls on each end before sucking me into her mouth.

She had a little trouble taking me into her throat the way I'd taught her to all those years ago but with time and practice we'll get back there. I fisted her hair as she fucked her face with my cock.

"I'm going to cum in your mouth. Don't worry I'll have plenty left to satisfy your pussy." I moved my hips back and forward faster and faster as she was able to take more and more of me into her mouth.

"Fuck baby." I leaned over her back and smacked her ass before feeling around beneath her until I found her pussy's hole. I slipped two fingers inside finger fucking her while she hummed around my cock that was ready to explode. When it hit I pulled back far enough to spill on her tongue. "Swallow." She made a face like she always did but she swallowed and then smiled before wiping the edge of her mouth.

I pounced on her forcing her onto her back and diving into her pussy face first. "Hmmm." I ate into her pussy sucking up all her juices as they escaped. Lifting her ass so I could bring her cunt closer to my mouth I spread her wider sinking my tongue deeper.

"Please Jake." Not yet I needed more of her taste, needed to get my fill before I fucked her long and hard into the morning. When she complained that she couldn't take anymore of my mouth I eased off and climbed up her body letting her taste herself on my tongue.

The kiss was hot and wild, I could feel the lust coursing through her body as she reached between us and took my cock in hand leading me to her pussy and pulling me in. I stroked her sweet pussy nice and deep making her cream all over my cock before pulling back. It was going to be a while before I came again.

I pulled out and ate her again. I would never get enough of her pussy; never. I ate her again until my tongue grew tired and her fingers were boring holes in my scalp as she begged me to end her torment and fuck her. She'd forgotten to be shy as she swore at me to fuck her pussy.

I slammed into her taking her mouth at the same time to catch her cry. She bit my tongue and fucked up at me, her hips moving wildly as she tried for her orgasm.

As soon as she calmed down I pulled her up to her hands and knees and slammed home again. This was the first time taking her like this, my favorite position. I knew this way I would be much deeper inside her.

Grabbing a fistful of her hair I slammed into her over and over as she spread her knees and pushed back at me taking my cock all the way into her womb, right where I wanted to be. Her ass was a thing of beauty as it jiggled with my every fuck and I couldn't wait to get inside. The thought brought me to the brink and I reached beneath her for her clit again to bring her off even as I spilled my seed inside her with a growl.

Chapter 12

Jake

The next morning she was literally sick at the thought of seeing her father. If I find out he'd been putting his hands on her

I'll lay his ass out. After a very long and rather satisfying night spent making love we fell asleep wrapped around each other. It was our first night together and our first as man and wife.

It was a whole new experience waking up next to the woman of your dreams. Feeling her warm breath on your skin, watching her face relaxed in sleep. She'd only had about four hours of sleep since we'd both had a lot of pent up lust to work off but we had to be on the road soon and I wanted this place behind me as soon as fucking possible.

I heard movement outside the door which meant mom was awake and stirring so I gave Jacqueline a few more minutes before kissing her awake. "Come on sweetheart, time to wake up." She stretched and frowned before turning back into my chest.

I decided on the best way to get her attention and turned her gently onto her back. She was sleep soft and dewy as I slipped my cock inside. I had to close my eyes for a moment to enjoy just the heady sensation of her pussy wrapped around me.

I could feel the swollen tissue from the overuse of the night before so no pounding, and she was definitely going to need a soak in the tub sometime before this day was over. Shit she was going to be on the back of my bike for the ride home. I could always let her ride with Mindy and mom but I was selfish, I wanted her with me.

"Umm, Jake…" She was moving beneath me before she opened her eyes, her legs spreading wider to accept me between her thighs. I buried my face in her neck and whispered.

"Good morning Mrs. Summers, did I tell you how fucking amazing your pussy feels?" That got her attention and she squeezed around me even as she lifted her legs up to hug my hips, her heels digging into my ass. When her fingers grabbed my hair and she aggressively pulled my mouth around to hers for a kiss I gave her what she wanted.

"Move faster Jake." She didn't seem to realize her tender state or if she did she didn't seem to care.

"No baby you're sore, if I move any faster it'll hurt and you need to be able to sit on the bike for at least the next six hours." She dug her heels harder into my ass and tried to force the issue so I smacked her hip to get her to behave. Big mistake; she threw her head back and screamed as she came all over my cock.

"Fuck babe from a tap?" What was a man to do or think the morning after taking a wife and he finds out she's even more what he wanted than he'd thought?

Three years of missing and needing her had given me plenty ideas. All those days and nights when I'd been stroking my meat to thoughts of her I had come up with some very raunchy ways to fuck her. Knowing that she liked a little rough play with her sex was just the icing on my fucking cake.

I didn't stop stroking into her but fucked her through her orgasm. I'd missed those sounds she makes when she gets overheated. Like a wild thing in heat, it was great for my ego to know that I could make the otherwise straitlaced, shy girl lose all control and give up her inhibitions.

I watched her face closely as I pulled her lower body tighter into mine and added some depth to my strokes. Still no pounding but I pulled out farther and farther each time before sliding back in. We rocked each other to a nice quiet orgasm, mouths locked together so we didn't give the rest of the house more of a show.

She refused to go to the shower alone, too mortified to face mom she said, so I went with her and we showered together where there was even more touching and tasting. I spread her leg over my bent shoulder and licked away some of the soreness from her red, swollen pussy lips.

"No more dick for you babe for at least the next few hours we have shit to do anyway you want to go say bye to your mom remember?" That's when she got sick and threw up and I wanted to strangle her asshole sperm donor.

"Babe if you're going to be this sick at the thought of going there I'm not taking you." She assured me that she was okay and that it was just nerves but I decided to keep an eye on her all the same.

I finished cleaning her up and then myself before taking her back to the room to get dressed. Mindy had snuck in while we were in the shower and left her a new top to wear.

After a quick breakfast with mom and Mindy where I made arrangements to have her car picked up, we headed out while they stayed to get their last minute stuff together. Mindy had been packing the stuff she knew mom would want to take with her all except her clothes and the old cabinet that had been passed down in her family from generation to generation.

My wife clung to me on the bike with a death grip and the closer we got to her old home the more I wanted to turn back. I didn't want anything upsetting her like this ever again but I knew if she didn't do this she'd regret it. I just wish it didn't hurt her this much.

We rode down the long driveway to the front door and I had to damn near carry her up the steps to ring the doorbell she was shaking so hard. Her father opened the door and went into automatic asshole mode. I don't think he had any other.

"What do you want? You're not welcomed here." I looked him in the eye and smirked. "Either you let her go see her mother or I will turn over every stone under which you've hidden your shit and be back in a couple hours with a warrant." He swallowed audibly but still had to play the big man to save face.

"Now." That got him moving when he realized I wasn't bullshitting. "Go on in baby and get whatever you want to take with you together, we'll swing by and pick it up when we're heading out." She actually had to sidestep him to get through the door, his last power play I suppose but I wasn't willing to give him even that. "Out of the way asshole before I knock you on your ass."

He turned to follow her inside but I pulled him up short. "You stay out here, go on and see your mom Jacqueline."

"I beg your pardon this is my home you have no rights here."

"Yeah but your track record isn't so good where my Wife is concerned so you'll stay your ass out here so I can keep an eye on you while she does what she came here for."

"You really think you're something don't you? I promise you that that badge of yours means nothing to me..."

"You remember what I whispered in your ear last night that had you turning white as a sheet? Well I lied; I already know everything there is to know. That's why when she comes back out here you're going to go into your safe and give her what's hers."

"I don't know what you're talking about." He looked everywhere but at me, it was hell realizing your enemy had the goods on you.

"Sure you do, you know her inheritance that her maternal grandfather left her? She's twenty one now so you have no more rights over it."

"I knew it, I knew that's why you came sniffing around my daughter."

"No asshole you're wrong, I didn't know shit about it until after I was here the last time. When I went back I did some research, I made it a mission to dig up every speck of dirt on you and I found plenty. Good luck getting out of that hole you dug yourself with that shoddy oil deal you fuck." He stepped back and looked around to see if anyone else was listening in.

"You can't...it'll ruin me."
"Give her her money, and before you try any of your underhanded tricks I know every dime down to the last penny that she's due including interest, so if you've been dipping into that pot you'd better figure out how you're gonna put it back in say, the next ten minutes. Now when she walks out that door you're going to treat her like a daughter and you're gonna go get what's hers and bring it

out here and put it in her hands respectfully or I'll take great pleasure in breaking your fucking neck."

When she came out half an hour later I'd already threatened him with everything I had. He was not to stand in her way if she chose to call her mom in the future, which I'm sure she'd want to. I had to glare at him to get the ball rolling.

"Uh Jacqueline I have something that belongs to you." He said it like he was having his tooth pulled but at least he wasn't yelling. "What is it dad?" Still so respectful, I knew that after all he'd done she still wished for even one small kernel of the love a man was supposed to show his daughter.

Asshole, that's okay, I'll just have to spend the next sixty years making up for it. He went in and came back out with a packet.

I could see how much it pained him to give it to her and I wasn't ashamed to gloat over it. She opened it up and started reading. "What is this?" I looked at him when he took too long to answer her.

"It's what your grandfather left you when he died, you were supposed to get it on your twenty first birthday I've been keeping an eye on it for you over the years." Yeah right.

"But what does it mean?" I could understand her confusion. There was a fuck load of zeroes at the end of that number.

"It means you're rich let's go we have to be on the road soon." She turned to say bye to the asshole but he turned his back on her and went inside. Good riddance. I hugged and kissed her while she kept staring down at the paper in her hand before leading her to the bike.

Chapter 13

We were on the road a few hours later thankfully, after getting everything squared away. Mom was driving Jacqueline's car while Mindy took hers, and they were following behind me. I'd thought to make it one straight shoot but it wasn't looking like that was gonna happen.

My wife was a little down because when we went back to the house to pick up the stuff she wanted to take with her the asshole wasn't there. Plus she was sore so it was looking more and more like a two day deal. It was great to finally put space between me and that place for the last time. Now I could look forward to the rest of our lives.

The next three months were going to be just her and I doing whatever the fuck she wanted to do while I did my best to get her pregnant. I'm obsessed with that shit for some strange reason. Maybe I was a little envious of my guys and their families who knows, I wasn't going to lose any sleep over it.

We stopped for a restroom break and to have lunch about four hours out. She was still sulking and I'd had enough. "Babe you've got to pull your shit together, your old man is never gonna change, the sooner you accept that the better off you'll be." She rested her head on my chest, her new favorite spot, and I kissed her hair. Mom and Mindy caught on and did their bit to draw her out of her shell and by the time we were ready to hit the road again she was stepping a little lighter.

We made it another four hours miraculously before we stopped for the night at a chain hotel. As tired as I was from the events of the past few days all I could think about was getting her naked. "You two need anything before we call it a night?" Mindy grinned and wiggled her eyes at me while mom smiled. "No son you go on I'm tuckered out myself and that nice meal we just had will more than keep me until morning."

"Maybe I'll go see what they've got going on around here."

"No you're not or I'll tan your ass brat now go to bed, mom keep an eye on your daughter."

"Come on Mindy and stop teasing your poor brother."

"Spoil sport, see you two lovebirds in the morning. Try to keep it down will ya." I made a playful step towards her as she ran away laughing. Jacqueline as blushing but smiling, progress.

We said our goodnights and I pulled her into the room that was blessedly across the hall from theirs. She could be as loud as she liked tonight and every other night after this come to think of it. "Strip."

"Jake I have to freshen up we've been on the road for hours." She tried sidestepping me but she was laughing so I knew she wasn't serious, not that that would've stopped me.

"No deal I want you hot and sweaty come 'ere." She squealed and evaded by grab but I took her down in the bathroom door. "This is where you want it? Fine." I pulled her jeans halfway down her thighs, released my cock and slammed into her from behind.

"Fuck it feels like forever since I had you." She pushed back onto my cock as she looked over her shoulder at me. "Fuck me harder Jake." Her knees were close together because of the hindrance of her pants so her pussy was even tighter than usual.

I watched my cock gliding in and out of her, wet with her pussy juice as I butted against her cervix. If I was hurting her she didn't let on and her chants of more, more, more just made me crazy with lust. I used her hips to pull her on and off my cock as I battered her. She stayed with me through three loud as fuck orgasms before I emptied inside her.

"Now you can take a bath." It seems like she gets friskier in the bathroom. She loves to play with my cock until she has me seeing stars and I had no other recourse than to turn her to the wall and nail her from behind again. When we were done this time I just lifted her out and took her to bed after drying us both off. "Time for bed we've got another long day ahead of us tomorrow."

"Goodnight husband." She turned up her face for my kiss.

"Goodnight wife."

"I like the sound of that, I can't believe it's real." She looked at her ring in the moonlight coming through the window.

"I like the way it sounds too sweetheart and I can believe it's real, I always knew it would be." There's no way I would've accepted anything else. We fell asleep wrapped around each other once more.

I turned to her in the middle of the night hard and needy. It's like I was trying to make up for lost time or some shit. Or maybe it was just the very sexy thought that she was mine to love as often as I want. She'd been asleep but was only too happy to let me have her. I teased her until she was ready to brain me as she threatened to do if I didn't get on with it.

I put just the tip of my cock inside her, crowned it and held still. With her legs spread and clasping my hips I ran my hands over her body starting first with a light brush of my thumb over her clit. I rubbed her until she was slippery, her pussy clenching around the head of my cock.

"Stretch your hands above your head, no not like that beauty, I want you to grab the bars."

Her small hands wrapped around the bars in the bed which made her back arch slightly, thrusting her breasts up for my touch. Bending over her I took her pebbled nipple into my mouth and sucked. I felt the answering twitch inside her walls as she clenched and released around my cock.

I teased her body to a fever pitch giving her just a taste of my cock before pulling back. On the next stroke I pulled out and climbed up her chest feeding her my length as far as it would go. She suckled me like a baby bird while I held her head in place. She loves having my cock in her mouth and I love putting it there.

I got into her throat and held still while she worked the muscles in her throat around my swollen cock. "Enough." I wanted to plant this load inside her, deep enough to do some good. Time to get started on some serious baby making.

I pulled out of her throat and kissed my way down her middle until I had her pussy in my mouth again. The maid was in for a surprise tomorrow when she changed these sheets; my cock was leaking pre cum all over the place.

When she filled my mouth with her sweet nectar I slid up her body and slipped inside her. "I love you Jacqueline Summers." She reached up for my mouth then as the bed rocked beneath us. Her hands were still clutching the slats of the headboard leaving her nipples thrust upward for my mouth. I bit into one hard to see if she'd like that and she almost broke my cock in half.

She started making those fuck awesome sounds again and I started pounding into her for all I was worth. "Oh yeah baby keep moving like that." It was a race to the finish as I slammed into her over and over again, visions of me planting my son or daughter inside her taking over my head. I wanted that now more than anything. "I'm going to breed you sweet Jacqueline right fucking now."

She liked that too because she yelled out her pleasure and came, dragging me over with her. I was done after that, I barely had enough strength to drag her back into my arms and pull the sheet over us. "Sleep sweet girl. Tomorrow you reach your new home and start your new life."

Chapter 14

My wife is a train wreck. She's all elbows and knees while she sleeps. I guess the night before had been a fluke, because tonight she almost kicked me off the bed twice. I ended up having to sleep with her under me with one leg over both of hers and my arm holding her down. That's the only way she would settle down. This for me though was not conducive to having a good night's rest.

My cock was in too close proximity and the feel of her breasts under my arm was a distraction. Out of concern for the long day she'd had on the back of the bike for the first time I didn't want to be a pig and wake her up again to fuck. So I stayed awake half the night counting down the hours. About four in the morning I said fuck it and just took her. I think this might become my new favorite thing. Fucking my wife while she sleeps. She's so malleable then, all I had to do was open her legs a little wider with my knee, bury my face in the sweet sleepy scent of her neck and slide into her warm heat.

"Jake?"

"Yeah baby go back to sleep." By now she was catching onto the rhythm of my strokes and moving ever so slightly beneath me. Not quite awake yet, she just enjoyed the feel of my hard cock inside her. This just might work in my favor after all because it was coming to my attention that she likes to do her own thing when we fuck, meaning she likes to run the show.

Sex is so new to her that she wants to try everything all at once. This way it's like I've corralled her little ass and I'm at the controls. Shit, spoke too soon. Her hips started moving a little faster beneath me and her nails were in my back. She's up. "Ooh that feels good Jake...you feel bigger and harder. I like it." She went after my neck because I think she'd pretty much figured out that if she wanted me to nail her hard that was the way to go. There goes my early morning slow ride.

"I want to eat your pussy before I cum

inside you, since you're awake…" I shrugged my shoulders even as I pulled out and lifted her to my mouth. I held her open with my hands spreading her and licked deep inside her pink flesh. She fucked my tongue while her head twist and turned on the pillow beneath her.

I love the way she moves, so sensual, she lets me know that she's enjoying whatever I do to her. "Cum in my mouth baby I need to fuck." I thumbed her clit while alternating between licking and sucking on her pussy, which was all it took to set her off. She came on a sweet sigh and relaxed back into the pillow.

"Jake?" Shit she wanted to talk, I'm coming to know her and that was her I want to talk voice, hopefully whatever it was won't take long or I could do it while we fucked. I laid next to her and stroked my cock while she got whatever it was she wanted to say straight in her head.

"Did you mean it, what you said last night?" What the fuck had I said? I barely had two working brain cells at this point.

She could ask me for the moon and my ass would try to get it for her if she'd just let me fuck; women.

"About?"

"Having a baby."

"Uh huh." She got up on her elbow and her eyes followed my hand as I stroked up and down. "So is that like the only reason we've been doing it so much?"

"Come again."

"Well after we you know, get pregnant, does that mean you're gonna want to stop?" Wow my girl really was innocent.

"When I fuck you baby it's always gonna be with a purpose, when I'm not trying to breed you, I'll be staking my claim, when it's not that it'll just be me showing you how much I love you now hop on up here." She climbed over me her eyes still stuck to my cock.

"But what if you…unghh…lose interest?" I took her ass in both hands and worked her up and down my length.

"Lose interest?" She was trying to look at where we were joined as she seemed almost fascinated by this new position. "Yes, in me." She finally figured out she could get more control by planting her hands on my shoulders and using her lower body to fuck me.

"Why…the fuck…would I …do that?" She's a fast learner fuck. She was testing out her new technique moving first one way and then the other.

"Because…you're you and I'm…me." She slammed down on my cock on that last word and really put some heat in it. I'm rethinking my favorite position here this might be it. "Don't follow babe." Good I could still form a sentence. She stopped all movement and I wanted to howl, my cock was thumping away inside her begging for release.

I finally looked at her face and she looked almost sad. What the fuck! "Because you're so beautiful and I'm not." She hung her head while I tried to make sense of what I'd just heard. I'm gonna kill that fuck, I'm gonna get on my bike and head back there and tear him limb from limb.

"Baby who told you that you're not beautiful?" She refused to look at me so I sat up brining our bodies closer together. Taking her head in my hands I brushed the hair back off her gorgeous as fuck face.

"I'm just not that's all, I have brown eyes and this." She took the ends of her hair between her fingers and scowled at it. "I've never even been to the salon to get it done, never had clothes like the girls wear. Daddy wouldn't even let me cut it."

Alright Jake she's serious here, how the fuck that could be was beyond me but I had to handle it right before I did more damage than good. "I agree with him on that at least, you're not cutting your hair I like it and if you want to go to a salon we'll find one as soon as we get home." Just please let me fuck. Bad husband Jake not cool; Okay.

"As to the rest, have you never seen yourself baby? You're fucking gorgeous, everything about you is. Why do you think I can't keep my hands off you? It's the middle of the fucking night and I'm ass tired but what are we doing? I get a whiff of you baby and my dick stands at attention. Let's get this out of the way so we never have to have this conversation again okay? I love your hair, your lips baby, fuck. I used to kiss you for hours don't you remember? It's because you have the sexiest mouth I've ever seen and your ass." I grabbed her ass for emphasis and pulled her up and down, kind of like a reminder of what we were in the middle of here.

"I want to fuck you every minute of every day because I think you're the sexiest, most gorgeous woman in my world." Success she was smiling again, blushing, but smiling. "Now can we get back to fucking?" She nodded and went back to work. I guess our little talk loosened her up some because she gave my dick a work out. I'm sure she didn't realize that I could see her magnificent ass in the mirror across from us, and boy what a sight it was.

It curled in and out as she fucked me, I could see my cock as it went up inside her and came out again. Fucking gorgeous. I spread her ass in my hands making sure to tickle her rosebud with my fingertips. "Baby I want to take you here." She looked down at me questioningly. "People do that?" Green, my wife is green as fuck and I love it. "Yes." She was breathing hard as she moved a little faster and her body became flushed. "Will it feel as good as this."

"Some women like it just as much or more." She stopped all movement and peered down at me.

"How do you know?"

"Babe, when we met I was twenty three years old and I know you've heard stories of my exploits when I was in high school so you know I wasn't a monk." What is it with women and this shit? Okay the fact that I would want to strangle every ex she'd ever had if there were any was neither here nor there.

"I don't like it." Oh she could be mean, she gave me one of those looks that if she'd had a weapon handy I would've ran for cover. "All that's in the past baby, now can we get back to this? All you need to care about is that I'm yours, all yours for the next sixty years you can take it out on my ass later but can we please get back to fucking? I'm dying here baby." She pouted but started moving again. I decided to help her out of her funk.

I wet the tip of my middle finger in her pussy juice and eased it into her ass up to the first joint. She almost broke my shit in half. "Yes Jake yes…" I guess that's a yes to the ass fuck in her future. She rode my cock hard as I enjoyed the ride, watching her movements in the mirror.

"Give me your tit baby." She didn't move fast enough, too caught up in her own pleasure, so I smacked her ass hard and that was it. She screeched and bucked and her whole body tightened.

Her mouth was opened in an oh as I pounded up inside all that tight sweetness while she shook herself to one hell of an orgasm. I kept that finger in her ass even though she did everything to break it and my dick. "Fuck this." I threw her to her back and pounded into her, pushing her legs back to her shoulders for deeper penetration.

"So good, so fucking good Jacqueline." She pulled my mouth down to hers and ate my face as her body tried to suck every last drop of cum from my balls. I was afraid I was hurting her with my hard thrusts but she stayed with me, her kisses wild and hot as she clenched her pussy around me and I lost it. The world ceased to exist; everything that I was was concentrated in that one moment as I spilled inside her with a roar.

Chapter 15

We got a few more hours sleep after that and then it was time to get on the road. Her ass was a little sore from sitting on the bike for so long so I had to work out the kinks, which led to a nice back shot with her lying flat on her stomach while I straddled her ass. I was too deep that way she said but she liked the little twinge of pain. This marriage shit just kept getting better and better.

I rounded up mom and sis and took my three girls to breakfast. The town we'd stopped in was only five hours away from home so I was hoping we could make it in one fell swoop but I was going to need their cooperation.

"Mom you slept okay?" we were sitting in a cute little diner with what looked like a mining crew taking up most of the tables. The place was lively and noisy with that air of hometown regulars who all knew each other and probably followed the same routine day in and out. I'm guessing my leathers and tats stood out among this bunch and that was the reason for all the stares. I preferred to think it was that and not my wife's ass. I wouldn't want to have to come back here later with my team and level the fuck.

"I slept just fine son I don't have to ask

you, you look…alert." Was mom zinging me? Jacqueline looked rather awake herself for someone who'd had my dick in her half the night. The waitress came over with a smile and was way too happy for fuck o' clock in the morning but I guess it comes with the trade.

"Good morning what I can I do for you folks this morning, start you off with some coffee?" We each ordered coffee and pancakes and eggs with turkey bacon.

"Okay listen up, I'd like to get back home some time this year so there will be no restroom stops every hour on the hour…" You'd have thought I yelled fire or some shit with the amount of racket that one statement incited.

I listened to their whining and bitching and then told them what was what. "Either keep up Mindy or I'll leave your ass behind, we should've been there already. Mom you're in a car so you're comfortable, my wife's on the back of my ride, which is not so much. I'm not making her do this three days in a row so everybody buckle down."

"She could always ride with me or your sister."

"Not gonna happen."

There was a lot of moaning and groaning, which only stopped when the waitress came back with three piping hot cups of coffee on a tray. I noticed Jacqueline sniffing hers and studying it like it was gonna bite.

"What's the matter baby, dirty cup?" She blushed and looked at the others before whispering in my ear.

"I've never had any before." I leaned away and studied her face to see if she was fucking with me. He couldn't have been that much of a dick. Who the fuck never had coffee?

"It's okay baby if you don't like it you don't have to have it you can have some juice." She bit into her lip and went back to studying her cup.

"I like mine with cream and sugar,

adds a nice flavor, he takes his black it's disgusting." Mom caught on and though she looked like she was about to cry for my girl she was very upbeat while she showed her how to doctor her coffee. Crisis over, she took her first sip and was hooked like the rest of the free world. I guess she was breaking down barriers one sip at a time.

With breakfast squared away I laid down the law once more before heading out. Three hours later we were at a rest stop. I didn't say shit just twiddled my thumbs until they did their thing and then got going.

We reached home around midday. They left me to drag their suitcases in while they went to look at the house. There were squeals and hugs and kisses and a lot of running up and down the stairs on both sides of the house.

Mom was a little more reserved but the two girls went wild. "You did good here son, and there too." She looked over at Jacqueline who was standing with her head bent close to Mindy's planning who knows what.

"She needs you...I had no idea." I pulled her in when she started to break down. "It's okay mom she's got us now to give her all the love she needs." I could finally breathe now, I'd done all that I'd set out to do. She was here and she was whole, and whatever demons chased her I'll fight the fucks myself. From here on out she was going to be as happy as it was possible for one person to be starting now.

"Alright listen up."

"Grrrrr, not another lecture."

"Pipe down Mindy, so here's the deal, mom after you've had a couple weeks to get settled in I'm sending you and Mindy to Hawaii for two weeks while Jacqueline and I go on our honeymoon." I got smothered with hugs and kisses for that one but it was all good.

Chapter 16

Jake

It was quite an experience watching her over the next few weeks. It was almost like watching a trapped bird on its first flight out of the cage. She was cautious but curious about everything, and the simplest things brought her the most joy. A simple thing like walking through town holding hands while eating an ice cream cone was like giving her diamonds.

My team had been sneaking me calls one after the other for the last few days, nosy fucks just wanted to get a look at my girl but they'll have to wait. I wanted her all to myself for now. Mom and Mindy were pretty good at giving us our space, which I greatly appreciated. It was our bonding slash breeding period.

Mindy spent so much time at the house

I was beginning to wonder if she wouldn't prefer just staying there instead of the condo, but I figured I'd let her make that call herself when she was ready. Their trip was set and all that was left was Jacqueline choosing where she wanted to go on our honeymoon.

Everyday she'd choose some place she found on the computer but by nightfall she'd change her mind again. I gave up trying to help about the fifth time she did that and told her she was on her own.

"I've got it Jake. The Grand Canyon, I've always wanted to go there, can we please, please, please?" It was the middle of the day and she was at it again.

"Fine but if we're staying stateside it's gonna be on the bike." She had to give that one a think but then she decided it was a nice trade off. "That's it? That's the only place you wanna see?" I knew it, she gave me her new make Jake stupid flirtatious look and climbed into my lap. This ought to be good; she's been trying out her wiles on me a lot lately. Who was I to tell her that I'd do whatever the fuck it was she wanted anyway? This way was much more fun.

My hand gravitated right for her ass while she straddled my hips. It was hot as fuck so I only had on jeans. I'd been watching her for the last half hour or so flitting from place to place rearranging our room to her liking.

I finally put my foot down the third time she had me move the chest of drawers. The movers had finally shown and she was putting her own personal touch on the place adding her shit.

"Well there're some other places I've read about that sounds interesting but can we just play it by ear since we're taking the bike?" She was one of those was she? Good for her.

"Whatever you want; you finished in here?" She looked back over her shoulder at the room before turning back to me.

"Yes I think so, for now." Thank fuck. "Where's mom and Mindy?" I hadn't seen them since breakfast, which seemed to be

JORDAN SILVER | 141

fast becoming a family tradition, having meals together. It was good that way because there will most likely be times in the future when I wouldn't make it home for dinner. This way she'd have company and not feel so alone out here in the middle of nowhere.

"They're picking out fabric for the window seats next door." She played with my chest and pressed her ass into my cock. Asking for trouble. I try not to fall on her like a starving beast every hour of every day but it didn't take much to perk up my boy's interest.

"You didn't want to do that?" I pushed her hair back off her face, it still amazes me that she actually thought she was plain. She has the most soulful eyes and like I said, her mouth is a thing of artistic mastery.

"I wanted to stay with you." So fucking sweet. I pulled her head down to mine and kissed her while feeling around between us to get my pants undone. "Hold up a minute babe." She lifted long enough for me to release my raging hard on. I eased her panty leg to the side under the little flirty skirt she had on and sat her down hard on my cock.

It was the slowest, dreamiest fuck we'd ever shared. Soft touches and whispers in between me working her up and down on my length. When I came it was long and drawn out with my lips fused to hers.

"I think it's gonna take me that whole sixty years to get my fill babe. Sweet." She can still blush, even after all the freaky shit I've introduced her to she can still blush like a teenage virgin. "Love you, now go tell your girls we're having dinner out tonight I feel like a big fat steak."

She wasn't done with me yet, she has this thing where she likes to use my left over hardness to get in one last orgasm. I let her ride the storm until she'd had her fill. "Okay." She pulled off my cock and went in the bathroom to clean up. My watch said it was still a few hours until dinner; good I can take a nap. I'm gonna need my strength for tonight because I'm sure she's gonna need servicing again.

I was out for a couple hours while I guess she was next door with the others. I'd had a very serious talk with mom about her relationship with my wife. Not that I expected her to mistreat her or anything but my girl needed a little more of what she'd been missing her whole life.

Mom was mom and I love honor and respect her but Jacqueline was my wife, I cling to her. Mom and sis are tight they have a serious bond and I just wanted them to let my wife in there somewhere since she was still feeling her way and this was all still new to her.

We hadn't discussed her inheritance as yet, I think she was a little intimidated, but she was gonna have to get to it soon. I don't trust Gary one fuck and the lawyer that was handling it after she'd turned twenty one was one of his cronies. I really didn't want to end up killing the fuck but I would in a minute if he hurt her again. Asshole.

We never talked about him which suited me just fine but she'd called her mom one day when he was sure to be at the office and they'd had a nice long chat. She told me it was the first time they'd ever talked like that. I don't even want to know what the fuck had been going on in that house.

Chapter 17

Jacqueline

Jake took us to this really nice steak house for dinner, after I'd changed like three times that is. Mindy had shared some of her clothes with me because I wasn't quite ready to go shopping yet. I didn't want to be away from Jake for even one second and he said being forced to go shopping with a female was grounds for divorce.

I tried my tricks on him and everything but he wouldn't budge. I guess that's a male thing, like a lot of other things I'm learning about him. He lets me do anything whenever I want no matter how outlandish. Like sleeping out in the backyard under the stars just because I'd never done it before and had always wanted to. Of course I spent a good portion of the night worrying about his mom waking up and looking out her kitchen window and seeing me on my knees with Jake pounding away inside me.

Sex is unlike anything I could've ever imagined, it's ten times better than in the books. The books couldn't describe that feeling you get when your husband looks into your eyes while he's buried deep inside you and says 'I love the fuck out of you'. Or the way he loses control and his body takes over and his nostrils flare as a red splash of color appears on his cheeks while he's cumming inside you. "What're you smiling at beautiful?" I reached up on tiptoe and kissed his cheek. "I'm just happy that's all."

We were waiting to be seated by the hostess and my mind had wandered for a minute. Was it any wonder? If not for the hour long baths he insisted I take everyday I would be too sore to walk.

Sex had become my whole life and I wouldn't have it any other way. We both approached it like we were making up for lost time. I think I'd always viewed marriage as what my parents had. Even when I knew all those years ago that I loved Jake I was quite willing to accept that fate if it meant I could have him for always. Imagine my shock that what we have was nothing like that.

Daddy pretty much ignored mom unless he was berating her about something she's done that was not to his liking. Jake meanwhile wanted to know everything I was doing every second. And he was such a mix of confusion, one minute he'd ask why I wasn't with his mom and Mindy while they were doing something next door, only to call me home half an hour later.

I think his job must be very tiring too because he slept a lot those first few days; the thing was I had to take naps too. I would lay there wide awake while he took his nap, then he'd wake up and pound me into the mattress before letting me go. When I asked him what that was about he said he couldn't sleep without my weight under him, it didn't feel right.

We were finally seated and Jake ordered me that drink with the embarrassing name right in front of his mom, because his sister the troublemaker said I liked it. He kept his hand around the back of my chair and I wondered when that would end? When he'd start taking me for granted and not want me as much…

"Whatever you're thinking wife cut it out." He whispered into my neck just below my ear. Did the man miss nothing? In the last few weeks he's been on top of everything. If I even hinted that I might like to try something he made sure I got it.

Except clothes, I wanted to try all the latest fashionable things in the magazines but Jake said he was just fine with what I'd always worn or as he'd put it. 'I fell in love with you while you were wearing that shit why the fuck you'd think that should change is beyond me'. And he'd thrown out my nice halter-top after tearing it in half. 'Too much of my shit on display in that thing

Jacqueline, I don't want to have to break a motherfucker in half for doing what comes naturally'. He has such a way with words my Jake.

"I'm not thinking anything."

"Yeah you were, it's written all over your face. You're worrying about some fuckery again, what is it this time?"

I played with my cloth napkin and peeked from beneath my lashes at Mindy and Joan to make sure they were busy talking to each other to pay any attention to our conversation. They were good about stuff like that. This way they wouldn't witness another one of my embarrassing moments.

I don't know why I keep acting like a ninny, this was everything I'd ever wanted, ever dreamed of. And maybe that's why I was so afraid that it would all end.

"Sometimes it doesn't seem real, that you could want me or love me this much." He looked over at his mom and sister before taking my hand that was laying on the table between us and putting it in his lap. My eyes flew open wide and I looked around to see if anyone else had noticed my husband putting my hand on his hard cock under the table."

"That answer your question? Now cut it out and enjoy your evening."

Just then we heard a child's scream and something crashing to the floor. Everyone turned at once to see what was going on. There was a very red faced woman sitting a few tables over with a very annoyed little boy who'd apparently thrown his food on the floor. The waitress looked stunned, like she had no idea what to do as the mother apologized profusely."

"Lady why don't you take that idiot and get the hell out of here? People are trying to enjoy a pleasant evening in a nice place nobody has time for your stupid brat." A very large man at the table next to theirs yelled loud enough for everyone to hear. The woman cringed with every word as though they were slaps. People at the surrounding tables started murmuring amongst each other but no one came to her rescue. I felt bad for her as she looked around as if afraid or ashamed.

"Son..." I looked up at Joan's call to Jake. I'd been so distracted by the young mother's turmoil that I hadn't even realized he'd stood from the table. "I'm good mom." My heart beat like a runaway train when he approached the beer gutted man who'd been accosting the mother. He looked like he could break poor Jake in half. Mindy was halfway out of her seat before her mom pulled her back down. "Your brother can take care of himself."

"Apologize to her." Jake's furious voice carried across the room, he was pissed.

"Who're you? Is that your brat? You people should know better than to..." He never got to finish whatever it was he was about to say because Jake picked him up by his throat. "Apologize and then you can leave."

"I have every right to be here this is a public place."

"So do they, they have just as much rights as

you or anyone else in here, except your rights have just been revoked…by me. Since you wanna act like a subhuman asshole you can go eat elsewhere now apologize before I make you."

"Sorry." He spat the words out before Jake flung him away like he weighed nothing. "Now get the fuck gone." The man scurried out of the restaurant seconds before the place erupted in applause.

Jake stopped by the table with the little boy and I don't know what he said but the kid lifted his arms up and Jake picked him up from his special chair. He must've invited them to our table because the woman looked over at us, and then back at him as if to ask if he was sure. Joan nodded her head at her and she got up and followed Jake and her son to our table.

"I'm so sorry and thank you for that. Andrew gets a little loud when he doesn't get his way he's autistic. He's not usually like that it's just he wanted Mac and cheese and they don't serve anything off the kid's menu after a certain time. I was late getting here and well…thanks. I'll take him away if he gets to be too much he sometimes takes a while to calm down."

"He seems pretty calm to me, besides my sister acts that way all the time and they claim she's normal." Mindy threw her napkin at him before saying hi to little Andrew who seemed fascinated by everything that was going on around him.

Jake

I should've broken that fuck's neck, this being a cop shit comes with its own drawbacks but I would've taken the hit for assaulting the dumbass, they ought to be a law. What the fuck is wrong with people anyway? If that had been my kid I would've kicked his ass into Outer Mongolia then followed him there and pulled his lungs out his fucking ass. Asshole.

The girls were all trying to involve Andrew in conversation. I was just trying to lighten the mood because his mom seemed a little frazzled. The last thing she needed was for some asshole to be hassling her like that. The waitress came over with some crayons and paper for him to play with and that's the only time he let go of my neck. I sat him on the seat between me and Jacqueline so he could color and when the young lady came back to take our orders I ordered his Mac and cheese.

"Sir we don't serve that after four pm I already told his mom…"

"Do you or do you not have Mac and cheese back there?"

"Well no it's made fresh every morning.

"You've got macaroni salad on the dinner menu which means you've got noodles, you have cheeseburgers on there too there's your cheese. Tell the chef to heat up some pasta and melt some cheese it can't be that hard."

"But sir…

"If you tell me about that four o'clock thing again I'm gonna lose my shit. That's a human being, that's a manmade device that keeps track of time. This kid has to go to bed hungry because that says so?"

She thought it over and came to the right conclusion, which was good for her and all concerned because I was seriously contemplating going back there and doing the shit myself.

"I'll get him his Mac and cheese even if I have to do it myself. It might take a minute…"

"We'll wait." Andrew was busy painting away, I guess he thought he was Picasso or some shit. He was handing out drawings to all the women the little shit, and flirting with my wife.

Dinner turned out okay Andrew ate his dinner and seemed happy enough. There were no more outbursts because he'd got what the fuck he wanted. I don't see what was the big fucking deal? I'm a grown man and sometimes I want to throw a howling fit. In fact if you asked my team they'd tell you I do that shit on occasion.

"You know that thing I was worried about earlier?" Jacqueline leaned over Andrew's head to whisper.

"Yeah?"

"I'm not worried anymore."

"Good girl."

Chapter 18

Jake

After dinner and it was time to go the women acted like they were long lost friends. Linda, the young mother spent a good five minutes trying to pay me back for her portion but I didn't even acknowledge that shit. She finally gave up when my wife and mother told her it was a lost cause. As we left the restaurant Jacqueline was stuck to my side while mom and Mindy walked behind with Linda and Andrew who was talking a mile a minute.

"Can you believe her husband left her because Andrew wasn't born perfect?" I kissed her head softly because her voice was so sad. After living with asshole number one she still didn't get it. "Babe everything with a dick ain't a man. No man would leave his family no matter what. In the long run they'll be better off without the fuck." She wasn't done yet because she was twitchier than a cat on a cross wire. Whatever it was I'll put her mind at ease however I could before she worried herself to death. My woman sure likes to worry about shit.

"But I feel so bad for them, she came all the way from New York and she has no family here, no one it's just so unfair."

"You learned all that in the last hour and fifteen minutes?" What the fuck is up with women anyway? It's like they meet each other and shit just starts spilling out.

"Well yeah, what's wrong with that? Anyway I think it's awful that she has to go through this and she has no way of getting back to her family, she's ashamed…"

"Where does she live?" She rattled off an address here in town, it wasn't the worst but it wasn't the best either. "I know where that it we'll follow them home." She squeezed my arm and laid her head on my shoulder for which she got another kiss to her head just because.

Linda once more tried to protest when

I said we were going to follow behind and make sure they got home safe. The women had already exchanged numbers so I didn't have to. I strapped Andrew into his car seat while he talked at me. I didn't understand half of what he was saying but I found out at dinner that as long as I looked at him and answered every once in a while with a yes or ok he was fine. Right now he had a whole lot of shit to say so I listened. When he was done I kissed his head and stepped back so Linda could do her thing.

Back in my jeep my girls were chattering away like magpies. Mom was planning a scarf and hat knitted set though the barometer was set to hell, I guess she was looking ahead to winter. Mindy with her teacher wanna be ass was trying to plan lessons or some shit, and Jacqueline was plotting something if the way she was going after her nail with her teeth was any indication. Me I just kept my mouth shut as we followed them home. I watched until she got inside the little house and turned on a light before waving to us out the window. My women had that place picked apart in five seconds flat.

"I don't like it, look at that place next door with all that old junk in the front yard."

"What about her yard it's too small there's no place for Andrew to run and play."

And on and on it went, I kept my damn mouth shut while the three of them rearranged that poor woman's life like she'd asked them to. "Look whatever you three are gonna do you'd better do it soon because we leave in two days." Shit the racket started then, apparently two days wasn't long enough time for them to stick their noses in people's shit and decide what's best for them. I took my life in my hands and offered up a suggestion.

"Why don't the three of you wait until she asks for help? She's an adult ladies and though I'd be the first one there with a moving van it's her call. Don't go overstepping boundaries." They let that settle in for all of two seconds before they ripped into me. "Honey her whole conversation was a cry for help, didn't you hear her?" My wife was giving me the pouty face. "No I was too busy trying to break Andrew's code the little fuck thinks he's slick." Tonight was the first time I'd ever had any dealings with an autistic child, never had any reason to before. But I have lots of experience with observing and deciphering shit, that's what I get paid hundreds of thousands a year to do. My brain is like some kind of machine or some shit.

What I got from Andrew is that everything he says makes sense he's just speaking in a different language. It's like some cultures read from right to left. Personally I think for kids like Andrew it's a choice, some people believer that we get to choose who we are before we come here. I don't know why the fuck that shouldn't apply to the autistic too. Maybe Andrew and his posse told the Big guy upstairs that they wanted as little to do with the rest of us humans as possible. Because from what I could see wasn't shit wrong with that kid, he's just a four year old with attitude.

"She won't come right out and ask for help son but we're women, we know what to listen for and she needs help." I went back to listening and keeping my mouth shut; whatever they needed me to do they'd let me know.

By the time we reached the house I think they'd pretty much figured it out. I'd heard bits and pieces but my mind had wandered towards our trip. I was trying to plot out the routes and shit, Jacqueline wanted to play it by ear and just go, sounds good to me but I'm not sure she's ready for that just yet. I'm willing to let her have her way for now though if it'll make her happy. "So have we decided how we're gonna disrupt this woman's life?" The three of them smiled at me all sweet and shit which was a dead giveaway. "Why don't we tackle that when we get back from our trips?" I guess mom was taking lead on this one, fine whatever.

We said our goodnights and once again Mindy was staying over with mom. Jacqueline still seemed a bit down in the dumps, which was not on my agenda for her so I'd have to do something quick. My baby is a worrier, not that she likes to, she just does. As soon as the door closed behind us I was on her. I cupped her magnificent breasts from behind, testing their weight in my hands. She sighed and leaned back against my chest while I opened her top and pushed her bra aside.

While sucking a hickey into her neck I pulled on one nipple while my other hand moved down beneath the waistband of her jeans heading for her pussy. I didn't forget those black silk thongs she'd put on earlier. It took a little bit of work but I found her pussy with my fingers and finger fucked her right there in the living room. Her ass rubbed against my already hard cock and I knew we weren't gonna make it into the bedroom. I lifted my mouth from her neck long enough to order her to take off her pants. While she did that I unzipped. She barely had enough time to get her jeans down her thighs and off before I was taking her down to the carpeted floor.

"I want your ass high in the air babe, this is going to be deep." She arched her ass high in the air for me while I rubbed my leaky cock head up and down her slit before pushing into her. "Ooomph…" I hit her end with one stroke and kept going. Sometimes, like now I just want to fuck the shit out of her, no finesse, no love taps. Just a balls deep pussy destroying fuck. I guess this would fall under the heading of staking my claim. Her loud cries only made me want to pound her pussy harder, so I did. Her knees skidded across the carpet and my dick followed, until I held her around her middle and fucked into her harder and harder. Her fingers had nowhere to grab so they scraped across the carpet with each pounding of my hips. The wet sounds of her pussy juice on my cock was sweet music to my ears as I watched it go in and out of her; and all the while she kept her ass nice and high for her man. "Fuck I'm cumming, cum for me baby." A finger in her tight ass was all that was needed to get her off and she squeezed the fuck out of my dick as I poured my seed inside her.

It didn't take us long to cum, but the night was still young. I felt a marathon coming on. "That was just a teaser."

I had to pick her up and carry her to bed, no

sense washing it off I since I planned to stay in her all night.

Chapter 19

Jake

The next day the women were buzzing around like worker bees getting ready for our trips. I ended up taking her shopping after all because I didn't trust the whispers and sneaky looks between her and Mindy. It would be fucked to have our first argument right before we left for our honeymoon but I knew there would be war if she came home with any of that too short shit.

"I like this one Jake." She pointed out something that looked like strips of material held together by some kind of metal loop in the back and from the way it looked on the mannequin would only come to about six inches below her ass. I gave her a look but she wouldn't back down. "You're out your fucking mind." She folded her arms and glared at my ass. "You've said no to the last three things I picked out, fine why don't you just choose for me then?"

"I thought that's why I was here."

I ignored her and went through the racks looking for stuff that wouldn't make my woman look like she was on the prowl or some fuck. "Jeans and tees." Sounded fine to me, besides she was going to be on the back of my ride a lot she would need comfortable shit. "It's hot in Arizona Jake can I just have some shorts?" She rolled her eyes which made me want to laugh. If she thought she was pissing me off with her sass she was sorely mistaken, that shit had the opposite effect. I loved the fact that she felt safe enough to speak her mind with me, unlike the way things were with the asshole. It meant she was slowly shedding those fears of hers which were the only flies in my ointment.

"How short is short?" I got a growl and a stomp before she went about her business and left me to mine. In the end she got a few new pairs of jeans and some nice tops with a couple pairs of shorts that came to her knees and something the sales lady called capris. She seemed happy enough with her haul especially since I'd let her go into the lingerie shop on her own. She could go as skimpy as she liked in there since that shit was for my eyes only which is just what I told her.

The next day you'd have thought these people weren't going to see each other again in this lifetime as much crying and I'll miss yous that were flying around. "Let's go baby the cab's here to take them to the airport." I'd had to repack her shit because I don't think she understood the concept of going cross-country on the back of a bike. Light was the name of the game but I guess she wouldn't be a female if she didn't try to take her whole closet with us.

We hit highway sixty-four a couple hours later and it was a straight shoot ahead. My baby had been good so far. She'd only needed one stop to use the facilities and she hadn't bugged me every hour on the hour about being hungry or sore, in fact she seemed to be enjoying herself. I had our helmets outfitted with speaking devices so we could talk to each other without having to shout over the wind and she yammered away at me all day. I loved it.

By nightfall we were pulling into the hotel and she'd had enough. "You did good baby I'm proud of you." She got a kiss and a pat on the ass for being such a good girl. She leaned on me while I checked us in and then we headed up to our room. "Room service tonight babe you're beat." She seemed to perk right up as she jumped on the bed and rolled around on it. "But I want to go look around."

"We can do that tomorrow, start fresh. You're gonna be sore in a few minutes believe me." I ignored her pouty face and went to run her a bath. "Come on sweetheart a nice hot bath and then room service." I had to undress her because she turned stubborn and refused to do it herself. Suddenly she was too tired to do anything. I took her into the bathroom and climbed into the tub with her in my arms. Turning her back to me I sat her on my cock and picked up the soap to wash her. "You have to hold still the whole time we're in here. If you're a good girl I'll reward you later." She fidgeted for a minute trying to force my dick to move inside her without moving too much, slick. I pinched her nipple to get her to behave. "No cheating brat." She whined and complained but held still.

That shit lasted two minutes for me though because she started tightening her pussy walls around my cock and I couldn't stick to my own rules. "Fuck you cheated." I pulled on her tits while rocking my hips up driving my cock into her belly. She'd made me hard as fuck with that shit she'd done. "Play with your clit for me baby I don't want to give up the tit." She reached down and I could just make out her fingers frigging her clit between the bubbles that were being displaced by our movements. "Fuck hold on." I stood with her on my cock and stepped out of the tub headed for the bed. I leaned her over the end of the bed and fucked her. Her ass was calling to me and I thought why the fuck not? Now was as good a time as any, shit where the fuck is my kit? I had to reach over her back to get my bag that was sitting on the other side of the mattress, which sent my dick deeper inside her.

"Ow." Shit I'd hurt her.

"Shh baby it's okay." I pulled out a little to give her pussy time to adjust. "You okay now baby?" She started moving on my cock again so I guess she was. "Uh huh feels good just...shocked me that's all." If she thought that was a shock what I'm about to do would surprise the fuck out of her. "What's that? It's cold." I'd come prepared with lube. I rubbed some into her ass getting it nice and oiled up for my cock which was growing harder and fuller with anticipation. I gave her no warning before pulling out and latching onto her pussy with my mouth. She's gonna need to be hot as fuck for me to take her ass without causing her too much discomfort.

"Umm I like your tongue." She reached back and grabbed a fistful of my hair while I tongue fucked her. When she came with a scream I stood behind her, oiled up my cock and pressed into her entrance. She tensed up a little which was to be expected but I soothed her.

"It's okay baby I'll take it easy just relax and let me have you here. Give me your tongue." I had to bend almost double to take her tongue in my mouth. I shoved two fingers in her pussy while easing ever so gently into her ass. When I had about five inches in she relaxed a little pushing back against the cock in her ass while fucking herself on my fingers.

I'd never been in anything so fucking tight in my life. Her ass had a death grip on my cock and when she reached beneath us and cupped my balls the growl that escaped me resounded around the room. I slammed all the way home I couldn't help it. Her ass sucked me in as we started a push and pull motion.

I was literally up on my toes as I tried to fuck her even deeper. Her screams were muffled in the sheets and I hoped like fuck they weren't screams of pain because I couldn't stop.

The looser her ass became around my cock the harder I fucked, it was never ending, just one long stream of pleasure pain so fucking intense I wanted that shit to last forever. Her soft hands on my balls put paid to that and I was soon growling into her neck as she flooded my fingers and came. I pulled out before I was finished in her ass and sprayed her back with what was left of the fuck load of cum in my nuts. "Fuck I love you, as soon as I can feel my limbs again I'll feed you."

Chapter 20

The next morning she was up early and raring to go, me not so much. It would be embarrassing for me to admit that my young newly initiated wife had worn my ass out. It was also safe to say I'd created an anal junkie. She'd experimented to her heart's content all night until my dick was rubbed raw. How she could be up and ready only a few hours later I couldn't fathom. I snapped open one bloodshot eye to peep at her when she started pushing my shoulders. "Come on

Jake it's time to get up the sun's coming out." Fuck she sounded wide awake and I needed at least two more hours.

She'd used my cock for her own pleasure all last night, it was getting so I was wondering if I'd ever get inside her pussy again she just wanted it in the ass. At about the fourth or fifth time I had to wrestle her onto her back and take it. "It's time to get back to my breeding program I'll fuck your ass again later." She'd pouted but had given in easily enough when I started fucking into her nice and hard. I guess she was happy enough with my efforts if her loud screams and the nails scoring my back were any indication.

Now there she was ready to jump out of her skin with excitement. "Jake come on I don't want to miss anything." What the fuck is there to miss? It's a hole in the ground that's been there for fucking ever and nobody knows how it fucking got there? What the fuck? "Not yet baby I need another half an hour." When she looked like she was going to protest I snagged her around her middle and pulled her down beside me.

Turning to my side I threw one leg over her hip and my arm under her breasts holding her in place. That might not have been such a good idea after all. One whiff of her scent and my boy went on the alert.

She started twitching her ass against my growing hardness and I bit into her neck to make her stop. "Cut it out." She held still for all of five seconds before she started up again. "Fuck, fine." I pulled her top leg over my hip and opened her up for my touch. She was bare beneath my shirt that she'd filched to sleep in.

All that expensive lingerie and she'd ended up in my old tee anyway which was fine by me. I knew what was underneath and that's what had my cock putting up a very valiant fight even though she'd tried to destroy him last night. I tested her pussy with my fingers, kind of like testing the waters so to speak. She hummed and pushed back against me. I dipped them lower and entered her liquid heat while teasing her clit with my thumb.

"Hmm Jake…" Her ass rubbed up and down the length of my cock while I fingered her. "Pull on your nipple baby." Her hand flew to obey as her body picked up speed.

Pulling my fingers out of her I slid down until I reached her legs. Scissoring them over my head I opened her up and licked her wet pussy from slit to clit. Her hand came down to grab hold of my hair as she tried pulling me harder into her pussy. She was smothering my ass but I didn't care, she tasted so fucking good it was almost worth it.

I couldn't open her with my hand because I was using it to stroke my cock, using the pre cum to ease some of the sting from the soreness. Then I got an idea. "Turn around." I had her turn to face me still on her side. "Suck." I fed her my morning wood while diving back into her pussy attacking her clit with my teeth and tongue.

"Hmmm." It was my turn to hum as she licked around my cock head teasingly before sucking me into her mouth. Her tongue felt cool and soothing against the heat of my cock as I thrust back and forth gently into her mouth. "Pull off." She took a few more swipes with her tongue before letting me go.

"Lay flat on your stomach." She hurried to obey probably thinking I was coming for that ass again but I had other ideas. Climbing over her I teased her opening with my engorged cock head before slipping in. When I was about halfway in I slammed the rest home and she lifted off the mattress.

"Stay." I held still, flexing the muscles in my ass and thighs making my cock twitch inside her. Planting my hands flat on the bed beside her I started deep stroking into her.

"Jake…" She sounded almost afraid. "I know, you can feel me more this way, it's okay I need this." She twisted the sheets in her hands and held on.

"Don't move, I want you to lay there and take it." I pulled out and slammed in again, she tried pushing back for more cock and I clamped down on her neck with my teeth until she settled down again. Lifting my back slightly away and arching my hips sent me deeper on my next stroke.

"Ouch…" I didn't stop moving at her cry of pain I knew it would hurt a little from this angle, but I did ease up a little. "Hurt?" She was grabbing the fuck out of the sheets and gritting her teeth.

"Yes…but…feels…good." She was my good girl and held still while I fucked her until I told her she could move. The only reason I'd told her not to was because I knew if she'd moved her ass the way she does, the way that makes her pussy give my cock a workout, it would've been over before it begun.

I growled like a beast as I came inside her clutching pussy and fell on her back fighting for my next breath. "You're killing me love." She wiggled her ass beneath me and grinned. Too much fucking energy in this one.

We joined the other hundred assholes on the train that takes you through the grotto. Then she wanted to take the helicopter ride. Next it was the damn donkey that looked like it would topple over under my weight. Love sure can make a man do strange things. She wanted to go up to the overlook and dragged my ass behind her. I didn't see the big deal we'd already seen it from the copter but this was her show, I was just there for ballast and to keep assholes at bay.

She was wearing some too tight jeans and had tied her tee shirt at her waist; huh. I don't recall okaying that fashion statement but it was too late to do anything about it now. Her ass in those jeans was like a magnet, which meant the men attached or otherwise were drawn. Some of them didn't even notice me standing there until I crowded her and gave them the fuck off glare. She soon caught on to my antics and thought that shit was funny. She wouldn't find it so funny if I threw one of the fucks over the rail. The third time it happened I whispered in her ear. "When we get back to the room you're gonna pay for this little wardrobe mishap."

Chapter 21

I let her drag me all over William's Junction for the next two days. After the crater there really wasn't much else to see. "Babe you had your choice of anywhere in the world, why not Greece or Paris?" I thought that's where all women wanted to go, the fuck I know.

She was lying on my chest in bed the night before our departure. We were both tired from trying to see all of Arizona in one shot. We'd ended up in Sedona for the scenery, which if you ask me was a better deal. That at least had been a nice two-hour ride through beautiful country. Now she's telling me her next stop of choice on our little honeymoon.

"I wanted to see home first, there're lots of things to see right here then we can go to those places later." Okay that made sense, but her next choice was Yellowstone in Wyoming a good ten or eleven hours away. When I suggested Yosemite, which was basically a stone's throw from where we were she said she didn't want to go there because they'd had an outbreak the year before. Fair enough. At least she was breaking out of her shell more and more with each mile.

I don't know if it's the desert air or what but she's wild. Every night as soon as we got back to the room she went on the attack. I no longer had to be the one taking her down because more often than not she was the one with her hand on my cock, teasing the shit out of me through my jeans. I also think we'd taken care of her little fashion rebellion.

I don't think she'd be trying that shit again anytime soon. I'd kept my word and spanked her ass that night. That, followed by her hardest fuck to date with no cuddle time after had shown her the error of her ways. Though watching her tearstained sad face was almost more than I could take. I'd come close to folding but in the end I held tough, until she fell asleep anyway and her pitiful sniffles had me turning to her and drawing her into my arms. I'm pretty sure she's going to be spoilt the rest of her life, the trick is to not let her know that.

I didn't see half the shit they promised at Yellowstone except a bear, which I wasn't interested in, but she loved it. She took a million pictures between the two places half of which was apparently for Andrew.

I hadn't heard his name until a the night before it was time to head back home. It was only halfway through her obviously well practiced speech that I realized they'd planned it that way. I was lifting her on and off my cock as she rode up and down in my lap. She'd sucked my cock until it was hard enough to hang shit on to dry. Then she'd teased the ever living shit out of me with her pussy as she sat on my face. In mid stroke I stopped all movement, she was halfway down on my rod. She might've started this as a game but she was all in now. Her nipples were pebble hard, her skin was flushed and her eyes were damn near rolling back in her head.

Now I'm willing to give my woman any fucking thing in this world without qualification, but the one thing I won't do is play fucking games.

"Jake what...why'd you stop?" She tried forcing the issue by moving her hips roughly but I held her still between my hands. "What're you doing?" She looked down at my question with her eyes still glazed over with lust. I guess it was going to take her a while to figure out she'd fucked up and the game had changed.

"What do you mean?" Still no clue, her only interest was in the hard meat stuffed inside her little pussy, too bad for her that shit was coming to a sudden unplanned end. I hadn't lost interest, I don't think that shit was even possible where she was concerned but I was beyond pissed.

"Who taught you to use sex to get what you want out of me?" I guess the harsh timbre in my voice alerted her to the danger and she finally wised up.

I lifted her off my dick; her guilty look was answer enough for me. "Jake I'm sorry I didn't mean anything by it." She scrambled off the bed to follow me but I slammed and locked the bathroom door.

A nice cold shower should take care of my needs just fine I didn't even want to finish in my hand. I never thought I'd be this fucking pissed at her in our whole life together and here it is just a few weeks in and already she's found something to piss me off royally. I let the cold water do its job, which wasn't as easy as I'd thought it would be. Imagining her pussy for the last three years didn't come close to being locked inside it so I had that working against me.

I left the bathroom and without saying a word got dressed and headed for the door. "Jake where're you going?" I didn't answer just took both keys and left. I needed to clear my head and she needed to think about what the fuck she'd done wrong.

I'm not too interested in what some talk show guru or afternoon TV nosy fuck says that's' just one man or woman's opinion. Dr. Dick can go fuck himself and who the fuck ever else spends an hour each day telling people how the fuck to live their lives can join him.

I'd be fucked if I'm letting them and their manipulative bullshit run my shit. I'll take every TV out the fucking house first if I find out that's where she learned that shit. I know she didn't learn it from my mom and she damn sure didn't learn it from hers. I guess I should be happy that she wasn't acting like she'd brought any of what she'd grown up with into our relationship but right now I was too pissed to see the bright side of shit.

A team doesn't work against itself. What the fuck kinda sense does that make? She'd been working her way around to telling me that they wanted Linda and Andrew to have the condo until she got on

186 | BAD BOY

her feet again and to get her out of the
neighborhood that they'd decided was too
dangerous.

Okay fine, Mindy liked it at the house
more than she liked it there alone anyway.
The place was paid off so Linda wouldn't
have to pay rent which I'm sure would be a
huge help for a single mom on her own. So
far so good though I wasn't sure what
Mindy was going to do when her boy Dylan
came out a few months later like they'd
planned. I guess they'd squared that shit
with mom, which was fine by me. They're
adults, she has an engagement ring on her
finger, it's all good. As long as mom's fine
I'm cool.

What I am not cool with is the way
she'd chosen to try to get me to agree. If
she'd known me better she would've known
two things. First, that I never stopped
thinking about little Andrew and the shit life
his dickless sperm donor had relegated him
to when he walked.

No security blanket, a woman and
child need that shit. I was always gonna do

JORDAN SILVER | 187

something about the situation. And two her scheme was the surest way to get me to say no to whatever the fuck it is she wanted.

I can't make my man Andrew pay for her stupidity though so I'm gonna have to come up with something else. It's a good thing we were leaving because it would be fucked to fuck up her honeymoon. Not what you want your woman looking back and remembering, but then again she'd brought this shit on herself.

Trying to manipulate me with pussy, did women really think all men were saps? Let's see how well she does without my dick in her belly. Fuck she's fucking with my breeding program.

When I got back to the room she was still sniffling in her sleep, serves her ass right. I stripped and climbed into bed behind her turning my back. She felt the indentation and woke up.

"Jake." I pretended not to hear her so she tapped my shoulder, I know she didn't know what the fuck she was doing with that shit but she was going to learn this lesson once and for all.

"Don't." I shrugged her off and settled in for some sleep, my dick could calm the fuck down too because the only thing he was feeling for the next little while was my hand. Suck it up buddy we've got a woman to train. Her soft weeping tore at me but I held firm, the next few days on the road was going to be hell. Having her wrapped around me for hours usually left me ravenous for her by the end of the day, now I'm gonna have to find a way to combat that shit.

I turned off my mike and the headphones with it the next morning when we climbed on the bike. All through breakfast she'd looked like a lost puppy and my heart hurt so fucking bad I thought it would stop on me but each time I thought of giving in and saying fuck it I remembered her riding my dick and all the while plotting to use it against me.

That put an end to that shit quickly. For the next two days every time she tried to talk I'd shut her down until she caught on and left my ass for at least the next few hours. But women are a tenacious bunch so she never stopped trying.

We were home a few hours before the others were due and I left her to go do her thing while I headed to my home office. The last hour or so on the bike with her little hands clutching at me were torture, sleeping next to her each night without fucking was more so, why the fuck was I doing this again?

I checked my messages because I knew my guys wouldn't leave my ass alone for three months, but unless they called with something urgent they were fucked. It was just a lot of bullshit chatter and from the way every last one of them spoke I knew they were doing it behind each other's backs; children.

I saw her come into the room out the corner of my eye and thought she was just coming to state her case again until her voice had me picking up my head. She sounded almost scared.

"Jake what's this?" I looked up at her and my heart stopped. Getting up from behind my desk as slowly as possible I started making my way towards her when all I wanted to do was run and snatch her away from the danger.

"Baby look at me." Her eyes flew to mine." No don't shake, hold your breath, good girl...don't look down keep your eyes on mine."

"I know baby it's okay I love you, just keep looking into my eyes. Remember how we had to wait for almost an hour for that damn geyser to shoot?" I kept talking to keep her mind off of what the fuck was going on.

Why did it feel like it took a mile to reach her instead of just a few steps? As soon was I was close enough I put my hand under hers and slowly took the bomb. "Go outside baby, open the backdoor for me and then go as far away towards the side of the house." She started shaking and didn't want to leave me. "It's okay sweetheart I'll be right there."

JORDAN SILVER | 191

I walked as carefully as I could out the room and down the stairs. From my quick glance I saw that it was crude, homemade most likely. I couldn't stop to think who just yet had to get this shit out of the house first.

She did as I asked and I walked out the back and placed it on the grass looking around for something to cover it. I didn't have the necessary tools needed to either detonate or break it down. It wasn't on a timer that much was obvious but I didn't know what I was dealing with and wasn't going to chance it. I found an old bucket and put it over it before pulling my phone and heading around front to get her. "Hector, I need you guys at my place with the bomb kit now."

"What the fuck?"

"We'll talk when you get here hurry, my wife is scared out her fucking mind move." I hung up with him and went to get her.

"Come 'ere baby it's okay." She was shaking like a leaf, I wonder if whoever did this knew their days on the earth had just come to a swift end? It must be fucked to know you're gonna die soon at the hands of a madman. "Where'd you find it sweetheart?" She was so close it was almost as if she was trying to crawl into my skin. "It was under my pillow, I went to change the sheets and I move the pillows first and..." A hard painful motherfucking death.

Chapter 22

Jake

It felt like forever before my team got here but in actuality it was only five minutes later. They came in hot, sirens blaring and it looked like the whole lot of them were on my front lawn including the pregnant one.

To fuck shit up even more the cab pulled up to offload mom and Mindy. I needed to go with my guys to take care of shit but I didn't want to leave her so maybe it was a good thing they'd shown up in the nick of time.

She was still plastered to my front, her hands clutching me for dear life. "It's okay baby you have to let me go to work now okay." Mom and Mindy dropped their bags and looked around at all the strange people.

"What's happened son?" I pulled them in too and welcomed them home. "There was a little situation can't get into it right now I have to go take care of something. It's around back under an old bucket." I told the guys as they got what they needed ready to go handle shit.

"Listen I want you three to stay right here for a minute." I went over to the van my people had just pulled up in and got what I needed. Heading into the garage I ran the wand over my truck looking for any surprises but there weren't any so I climbed in and pulled out.

I wasn't sure what I was dealing with here but I didn't want to leave my wife out in the open just in case. "Get in the truck and stay there until I come get you." They tried arguing with me but it didn't take much to shut them down. Mom was already doing her thing hugging my woman and trying to calm her while Mindy brushed her hair with her fingers.

I put them in the truck and went to see where my people were at with this shit. I had to put a leash on my emotions and clear my fucking head.

The robot was doing her thing while the team stood a fair distance away. Tessie was a nifty little toy that DHS had paid millions for we have two of these shits. They can do in seconds what it would take a human minutes or sometimes hours to do. She evaluates the potential threat and dismantles it all by herself.

If the rest of the world really believes that Americans are the dumbest fucks on the planet they've never seen inside the mind of a homegrown MIT grad. This little beauty was the brainchild of a fucking teenager. He learned the shit from programming video games of all things.

"What the fuck boss?" My guys were pissed but they were nowhere near my level. I didn't let my mind play the guessing game that was no way to go into an Op.

If I started thinking it might be one asshole and focused entirely on him then I might miss something. I'm a free market thinker everyone is suspect except the three women sitting in my truck. If the fucker was watching this play out he was gonna need a rocket launcher if he wanted to fuck with them.

"Task complete." Who the fuck thought of giving Tessie Marilyn Monroe's voice anyway? That shit was just off. We walked over to where she'd picked apart what turned out to be an eight-inch metal galvanized pipe bomb.

You could buy that shit anywhere and so too the caps that were used. There were nails, which were supposed to project on impact and some fuck had put it under my wife's pillow. There was no timer it had been rigged to go off when she put her head on the pillow.

"Okay now we need to comb the house, both sides." We waited out in the van while watching Tessie do her thing going through the house meticulously step by step.

"Clear." The first floor was clear now we watched as she climbed the stairs. I looked over to the truck where the girls had their faces up to the windows.

"Melissa what're you doing here?" She looked like she was ready to pop any minute. "I'm part of the team aren't I?" Hardheaded fuck, I looked at her husband who just shrugged his shoulders and went back to watching the screen. Pussy whipped motherfucker.

When it looked like the house was clear I walked over to the truck while Terry went to get Tessie so she could do the same thing next door, I wasn't taking any chances. I climbed in back where my woman was and pulled her into my arms for a hug and a kiss to the temple. It had been days since I'd touched her with tenderness.

"You hanging in there baby?" She nodded against my chest and hugged me close. "How about you two you doing okay?" They were scared but holding their own. "We should be done here soon then you can go in and take a load off."

"Jackie said there was a bomb Jake who would do such a thing?" Mindy is one of those females that's going to be just like Melissa when she grows up. She was pissed and barely holding onto her temper, which I'm sure was only for mom and my wife's sake.

I had a pretty good idea who she thought was responsible but I wasn't going there and especially not in front of my woman. When whoever it was came up staked out on a pike somewhere she didn't need to know it was because of this or that it had been at her husband's hand. Women have strange ideas when it comes to shit like that.

"We don't know anything yet sis, don't worry about this shit just go inside when I give you the all clear and talk about your trip or some shit. Jacqueline took a million pictures to show you two and I'm sure you've got your own cache. That's all I want the three of you thinking about right now the rest of this is not for you." She opened her mouth to argue but I shut her down.

There was a knock on the window and I kissed my woman before stepping out. "It's clean boss what do you want to do now?" I opened the truck door and told the women to head on in while I go to my place to take care of something.

Melissa opted to go with them, which was a weight off my mind. They were already talking babies by the time they reached the first step.

"Okay I have to go look at the tapes, we only just got back literally so I didn't even think of looking at that shit. Had I done that shit she wouldn't have almost…fuck."

It hit me then, gut deep and hard. I could've lost her today.

I could be standing over her dead body in the fucking morgue right now. And for what, what had she ever done but be mistreated her whole fucking life?

"Easy boss easy." Hector's voice came to me almost from a distance, at least that's what it sounded like which made no sense. My hands hurt and I looked down to see blood dripping from the right one. What the fuck?

I'd punched the fuck out of the truck and had no recollection whatsoever of doing it. Without another word I turned and walked away towards the house with my team bringing up the rear.

In my security room I rewound back to the day we left. I didn't want to see the last hour, never wanted to see my wife picking that shit up from the one place she was supposed to feel safe.

It was the day before yesterday that we finally saw movement. Two things registered at once. One, how the fuck did this asshole know when we were coming home? I hadn't given anyone that information. And two, this fucker knew me or about me because he kept his face well hidden the whole time.

He came in through the back, I couldn't see what he used to jimmy the lock but he'd been smart to come in that way. If he'd used the front I would've noticed right away. I watched as he walked up the stairs sure and steady, he knew no one was here. How the fuck had he got pass my security? I'll have to look into that later.

He looked around the room still with his face hidden, what was he looking for? He walked over to the side table and picked up the book she'd left there. That's when he lifted her pillow and sniffed it before planting his little welcome home surprise.

Nail in his fucking coffin, he'd targeted her. "Show me your face you fuck." He was completely covered from head to toe. He wore leather gloves and his shirt sleeves were pulled down so there wasn't even a flash of flesh showing. Then he did it, he picked his head up as he looked around again. "Gotcha you fuck."

"Are you shitting me?" The room erupted as I sat and seethed, this complicated things but not by much. Some way somehow he was done. I reached for the phone on my desk; it was picked up on the first ring.

"Boy you're supposed to be gone for three months don't tell me you're bored already I told you…"

"Supe I just watched Samuels on my security planting a bomb under my wife's pillow." He stopped talking in mid stride. "The fuck you say." I gave him the particulars and can't say I was surprised by his first words to me.

"Jake you can't kill him." Of course he would know that that's where my head was at, he knows me better than most. He should also know that what he was asking was damn near impossible for a man like me. "That your only stipulation?"

202 | BAD BOY

"I'm pretty sure I can't stop you from going after him so yeah. Why do you have cameras in your bedroom anyway?"

"It's part of the house, it's where my wife sleeps why the fuck wouldn't it be the most protected place in the fucking house?"

"Okay son calm down I'm not the enemy. Look can you hold off on whatever you're planning? Let me try to work something…"

"Negative Supe, you fuck with me on this it would be the end of us, we clear? You don't do shit that would tip him off."

"I think you forget that I'm your boss."

"I think you forget I don't give a fuck, he gets away I'll level this fucking town to the ground."

"Okay, okay, calm down I wasn't going to tip off the fucker, I'm just trying to figure a way to do this so you don't get any flack from the big guys."

"You think I give a fuck about that either? And Supe about your stipulation…he's fucked." He was still calling for me when I hung up.

Chapter 23

"What's our play boss? What're we doing?" I looked around the room at all of them, all ready to go to battle for me but I couldn't and wouldn't ask them to.

"We're not doing anything I am. Not your fight boys." They let that settle in for a minute before they decided by their code what they were gonna do.

"We understand that you're pissed boss so we'll let that insult slide and not tell you what an ass backward shit fuck thing that is to say. Now how the fuck are we coming after this asshole?" Shit the last thing I need is a bunch of hot heads on my ass.

"This isn't business as usual boys this shit is personal…" Of course Melissa chose that moment to walk into the room. "Well, who the fuck are we hunting?"

"You're not hunting shit, Jace seriously can't you have her admitted for observation or some fuck? Melissa you're about to have a baby, the last thing you need is to be running around like fucking Shera. I could've sworn I put you on the desk more than two months ago; and don't think I don't know about you sneaking into Ops. The only reason I left that shit alone was because they weren't too dangerous and I knew the guys had you covered but this shit is different." She totally ignored my ass as she turned to her husband and the rest of her teammates.

"Who was it?" What the fuck? Did no one listen anymore? You leave for a couple weeks and everything goes to shit. "Samuels." Terry the fuck had no compunction about telling her, that's what happens when you build a team like mine.

They stick together no matter what to face all comers. Too bad I'd forgot to tell them that shit wasn't supposed to be used against their leader. "Stand down all of you, I'm doing this shit alone." My hand was starting to hurt like a son of a bitch and I looked through my desk for something to clean it up a little.

"Where is he usually this time of day? His office most likely, can't take him there too many eyes and heat." She was already planning strategy, my words going totally ignored.

"We can get to his car in the parking lot, he likes that cushy spot away from everyone else maybe we can use that in our favor." Mason one of the quieter of the bunch spoke up.

"I'm thinking the boss might want to make this one up close and personal."

"The boss would like all of you to stand the fuck down Hector." It was as though I hadn't even spoken, they just went on about their business discussing the best way to take out the captain. "We can't let you do that boss, your rules remember? If it affects one it affects all." Shit.

I sat back and listened as they threw around ideas. There was no point in arguing any farther they'd proven that. While they talked I formulated my own shit in my head. I pretty much knew what I had to do just had to figure the shit out. When the dust cleared I needed to be able to come home to my wife.

"Okay guys we're gonna need to pick this up tomorrow I have to go see to my woman." They looked at me suspiciously but I wasn't giving away shit. They're hard yes but I'm harder. I finally got them to leave by telling them Jacqueline needed me right now and I couldn't think about what needed to be done until I'd made sure she was okay. I played to their earlier assessment that I was too close to the situation, but the reality was somewhat different.

As soon as they were gone I went next door to get her. I had to give mom and Mindy some type of explanation but I watered it down as best I could. All they needed to know was that they were safe. My only thought right now was getting her home and alone. I needed to feel her under me, to reassure myself that she was really safe. I needed to wipe my mind clean of the image of her holding a fucking homemade bomb in her hand shaking with fear.

She started fussing over my hand on the way over but I couldn't even feel the pain anymore. "Jake you're hurt what did you do?" I looked at the swollen mess and put it out of my mind. I'd already ascertained that it wasn't broken just badly bruised, besides I had more important things on my mind. "Don't worry about it now baby I need you." I picked her up at the door and took her upstairs. Bypassing our room I took her to one of the guest rooms and closed the door.

"Jake." I kissed her to keep her quiet, I didn't want to talk about anything right now, I just wanted to feel. I unbuttoned her shirt and pushed it off her shoulders. Her bra was next before I unsnapped her jeans and pushed them down her thighs.

I left the scrap of material covering her pussy for last while I shed my own clothes with her help. Pulling her over to the bed without a word I laid her back with her ass hanging over the edge. Finally I pulled her panties off and inhaled her scent.

I'd missed her smell in the last few days, never again. Opening her up with my thumbs I took a moment to enjoy the pink softness of her flesh. She was already wet, beads of her essence just waiting for my tongue.

I licked her first before taking her clit into my mouth. I had to close my eyes against the pleasure that coursed through me as her taste burst on my tongue. Lifting her ass in my hands I left only her shoulders resting on the bed and ate her like I'd been starved for the taste of her.

"Jake." Her body shook as I took everything I needed from her. My cock was aching and full, pre cum dripping down to the floor when I finally let her back down. I pushed her farther up onto the bed and climbed over her.

Taking my cock in hand I led it into her soft heat until I was seated to the hilt. I held still, enjoying the feeling of having her hot pussy wrapped around me again. "Never again." I hadn't meant to say the words out loud it was a promise to myself that no matter what I would never deny her again.

Never keep what was hers away from her. It felt like forever since I'd been here since we'd danced this dance. She looked up at me with need clouding her eyes, her sweet face so precious.

An uncontrollable need rose up in me, the need to completely take her over. I wanted everything that she had to be mine, needed to own, to possess all that she was.

Lowering my head I took her mouth and kissed her slowly, taking my time to suck her tongue into my mouth while my cock stroked in and out of her slowly, deeply. My body wanted to fuck but I needed to make love to my wife. Not only because I hadn't touched her in days but because after today she needed it, we both did. I used my body to show her just how fucking precious she was and to erase the horror of what she'd been through.

She came for me twice, calling out for me to love her faster, harder but still I held back. I wanted to last, at least until I was over the image, until my world was set to rights again. If I could've molded her to me in that moment I would've. The love I felt for her as she moved beneath me was stronger than I've ever known. For three and a half years I loved her, thought I knew what love was, what that all consuming feeling I had meant. Until today, until I'd felt fear unlike anything I'd ever known.

The loud banging of the headboard against the wall brought me back from the place I'd gone to in my head. I shook myself back to awareness to realize I'd fucked her halfway up the damn headboard, her neck was at an odd angle and there was a huge red mark on her neck where I'd sucked her skin too hard.

"Fuck baby I'm sorry." I tried to pull out, to repair the damage I'd done. How else had I hurt her while I'd been lost in my own fucking head? She clutched at me and pulled my head down as her body moved wildly beneath my still thrusting cock. I'd come to in the middle of her orgasm, her body was still clenching hungrily around my cock. She shocked the fuck out of me when she wrestled me to my back and took over.

She was gone, somewhere primal and lustful. Her hips moved like a piston as she rode my cock up and down. Her head was thrown back and her mouth opened in surprise and all I could do was hold onto her hips and enjoy the ride. I didn't even try to take over just let her have her way. Until she fucked me so hard I thought she would hurt her little pussy.

I understood her need to feel alive, to feel in control but I couldn't let her hurt herself. When she lowered her head and I saw the tears she broke my fucking heart.

"Shh baby don't, come 'ere." I pulled her down to my chest and rolled us over. Taking her face in my hands I brushed her hair back and looked into her eyes as my hips kept up their movements.

" I love you Jacqueline, nothing's going to hurt you I won't let it." She strained against me too far gone to do anything more than seek her release. I needed to calm her so I pulled out and sucked on her pussy again until a few minutes later her breathing calmed and she stopped moving so wildly.

My heart was racing with my own need as I once again climbed over her, but this time it was I who needed. I turned her onto her hands and knees leading my cock into her weeping opening once more. Pounding out my love inside her as she cried out and begged for more.

We spent the night locked together in one form or the other. She even got her ass fucked when I was calm enough to do it without hurting her. When she was too tired and too sore to take me anymore for the night I took her into the shower and cleaned us both up before putting her to bed.

"Did mom feed you sweetheart?" Fuck I'd forgotten to feed her. "Not hungry sleepy...love you Jake." She wrapped her arms around my neck and fell asleep just like that. "I love you too precious girl, more than you'll ever know."

I waited until her breathing grew deep and her body relaxed in slumber before slipping from the bed. In the downstairs bathroom I cleaned and bandaged my hand flexing my fingers to test their dexterity. Should be good enough for what I had to do. Sneaking back up the stairs I took one last look at her lying curled on her side, the pillow I'd just left clasped to her chest. Turning away I headed down the stairs and out the back, it was best that I walk this one.

Chapter 24

Jake

I stayed to the back roads for the twenty blocks or so it took me to get to where I was going. The night was clear with not a cloud in the sky. And though it was a quiet, upscale neighborhood I kept my hoodie pulled down as low as it would go, walking as swiftly as possible without looking too suspicious. It was the middle of the night so most places were in complete darkness, only a few had the glare of a television showing through the shades.

I reached my destination and pulled my backpack around front to get what I needed. It took less than five seconds to get through the security and five more to pick the lock on the door. There was a soft glow coming from what I assumed was the living room.

I'd never been here before but I knew enough to know who the occupants were. That was the only problem, getting around the witness. I have no wish to end an innocent life but neither do I wish to spend the rest of my days in a federal prison. I felt my way along the wall until I reached the stairs.

I tested each one for noise before stepping up. There were four rooms on the second floor so using my keen senses I deciphered which one I was looking for and headed in that direction.

I eased the door open and went in low assessing the situation. The two occupants slept on their sides with their backs facing, one snoring. Reaching into my pocket I retrieved the syringe with the sleeping aid, better safe than sorry. She barely made a sound when I slipped the needle into her arm but I didn't wait for it to take effect; in and out.

Making my way around to the other side of the bed I pulled the fucker out of it by his neck. "Get up you fuck." He fumbled around between sleep and wake as I dragged him from the room out the door and down the stairs.

"Who are you, what're you doing in my house?" I pulled the hoodie off right before punching him in the throat and crushing his larynx. While he clutched at his throat and stumbled around I pulled my weapon of choice from the black leather backpack.

I had no need to speak to the asshole, besides he'd never be able to utter another word in his fucking life anyway so what's the point? As he laid on his living room floor trying to breathe I stood over him and lifting the high powered nail gun shot him in both hands and knees exactly where I knew they would do the most good.

I chose nails instead of bullets for the obvious reason that this fuck had tried to put nails in my wife's head. I guess I had something to say to him after all. "Fuck you." I turned and walked away as the stench of his body's release filled the air. Pulling my phone as I left I called Supe.

"You've got clean up, the wife should be out for another few hours." I could hear movement on his end which sounded like he was getting out of bed. "Shit Jake he breathing?"

"Barely." I hung up since there was no more left to be said. He got what he wanted, Samuels was still alive. The fact that he would never walk, talk, or use his hands again was gonna have to be enough for me. That and the destruction of his name after I get through digging up all the shit he'd been up to.

I jogged back through the streets towards home only instead of going around back I headed towards the front. The van was just where I expected it to be, hidden out of sight. These fuckers forgot I trained them.

I walked up and knocked on the side window and almost scared Hector to death. He rolled down the window with a grin. "Hey boss, nice evening isn't it?" I looked inside to see all of them, except the pregnant one thank goodness. At least her husband had some control over her after all.

"My ass Hector you hardheaded fucks can go home now." They looked around at each other and then all eyes turned to me. I didn't need to give them any explanations they knew. They nodded in unison and I turned and jogged back up my driveway to home and my wife.

Epilogue

Jacqueline

"Jake's gonna have a conniption fit." I looked around the room at all the chaos and clutter, and the people scattered around my living room. My mom was one of those people, which made me smile.

After Jake had taken over my inheritance because I kept dragging my feet he found out that daddy had been stealing from me for years among other things. He'd told me only once 'stay out of it' and had proceeded to destroy the man that had made my life a living hell.

Daddy was now incarcerated, the sheriff's department had been completely overhauled with quite a few of the old members now sitting behind bars for accepting bribes and using their office to terrorize the small town. Things that I hadn't even been aware of had come to light. It had gotten so bad that the government had sent in their own team of men to take over until honest men and women could be found to replace them.

Jake had given mom the choice of whether or not she wanted to stay there alone, move somewhere else, or come to our town. Since the new baby was coming she'd opted to be near us, and her grandchild. She'd found a house not far from us and was very happy there.

She wasn't the same cowed woman I'd always known though she still sometimes looked to Jake for direction. He was very patient with her and the two of them had formed a bond, only after I'd spent months convincing him that she hadn't really played a part in the way my life had been and that even if she did she was as much under daddy's control as I had been. He's not the most forgiving sort so that argument hadn't held much sway but eventually he'd started coming around.

My due date was just a week or so away and according to my husband I wasn't allowed to do anything more than sit somewhere quietly until he got home in the evenings.

"Melissa Troy's trying to eat the eggs again." I laughed at the antics of her little boy who was toddling around the room after filching yet another Easter egg from the table and going off to hide.

"He's just like his dad, greedy; give me that you little pig." She took the pastel blue egg and placed it back in the basket. Linda and Mindy were in charge of hiding the eggs later around the property for

Andrew's classmates to find tomorrow on the Easter egg hunt that we'd organized. Before Jake left this morning he'd told me in no uncertain terms that I was to do nothing, to let the others do it all and they were supposed to do it at Linda's place. Where I couldn't be because I was no longer allowed to drive according to him and no one else was allowed to drive me anywhere but him.

Did I mention that he's gone off the deep end?

Somehow everyone had gravitated over here anyway and in the end they'd just gone ahead and used our kitchen. There were at least six-dozen eggs that had been boiled and dip dyed.

Now we were stenciling little pictures onto the sides. I didn't know we would make such a mess and Jake was due home any minute so there was no way to clean up or hide the evidence before he got here.

To the average sane person painting eggs will not be seen as a taxing exercise but to my husband who seemed to have lost his mind in the last few weeks it would be the equivalent of lifting stone slabs of concrete to build a wall.

I've never heard so many don'ts in my life. If it were up to him I would only breathe while lying flat on my back and that's about it. The only time he let me move is when we were in bed and even there he had tried to curb his enthusiasm, thank goodness that hadn't worked out. He was

JORDAN SILVER | 223

fascinated with my body, he'd spend hours playing with my growing stomach which always led to more fun times for me.

Life had pretty much evened out after the whole bomb scare. The next morning when I'd woken up I noticed a difference in Jake. He was overly attentive and sweet, not that he hadn't been before but for the next few weeks he all but smothered me and I noticed that he would bite his tongue a lot when I did things he didn't approve of.

So of course I pushed the envelope because I kinda missed his bossy take-charge ways. I didn't let on that I knew what he was doing. He felt guilty about the whole situation and his way of making up for it was to let me get away with murder basically.

You would think I would appreciate that after living with a tyrant my whole life but I found myself missing his growled orders. I wanted to bash him in the head when I purposely disobeyed him one day and all he did was leave the room. I gave a lot of thought on what to do to bring him

224 | BAD BOY

back to his senses and found the perfect thing.

Mindy decided that she Linda and I needed a girl's night out so we went shopping. I bought the skimpiest most scandalous dress I could find. Of course I bought the dress that I was really going to wear that night because I wouldn't be caught dead in the thing in public, but I needed to get a rise out of Jake. I bit off more than I could chew that night though, though the memory still makes me blush.

"Where is it that you three are going again?" I was putting on my makeup while wearing a thong and thigh highs. I'd already put on four-inch heels because I was setting the scene so to speak.

My heart was beating a hole in my chest because there was no telling how he would react to what I had planned. If he didn't do anything this time I was at a lost as to what to do next. "It's a club, you sure you don't want to come with us? Your mom can watch Andrew."

Andrew had formed an attachment to Jake in the last few weeks since we'd moved them into the condo. The two of them were a sight, the big gruff biker with his shadow walking behind mimicking everything he did. Jake was so kind and patient with him it gave me goose bumps. I couldn't wait to see him with our own kids some day. I'd missed a period but haven't said anything as yet because my body has done that before due to stress, but I was hopeful.

I walked over to the closet and removed the dress I'd kept hidden from sight and stepped into it out of his view. When I walked back into the room I pretended not to hear his indrawn breath. I held mine waiting to see what he would do and was about to give up hope when a few seconds slipped by without a word. But then I'd felt his hands on me and the next thing I knew the dress was torn in half and lying in a heap at my feet.

"What's your second choice?" I looked over my shoulder at him with my mouth hanging open, his face looked like a thundercloud. It was all I could do not to break into laughter but that would spoil the whole plan.

"Jake…" He pushed me back against the wall and put his hand around my throat. Uh oh, maybe I'd gone too far.

"Where the fuck did you get that shit? Did you really think you were gonna walk out of here in that?" I tried calming him down but he was off and running.

"I've let you get away with shit because I was trying to show you how much I love and appreciate you and you've done plenty in the last few weeks to push my buttons but this is the fucking limit. You're not going anywhere now, in fact it would be a fucking miracle if you ever leave this house without me again if that's the type of shit you're gonna be wearing."

He didn't stop there either, after ranting and raving he'd called Mindy and told her to go on ahead without me. I'm sure she'd understood because I'd let her in on what I was doing but she'd given him a hard time on the phone and he'd hung up on her.

"Get over here." I wanted to run and jump on him but I couldn't seem too obvious. He'd just torn my new dress I had to show him how pissed I was. I walked as slowly as I could over to where he now stood next to the bed.

"Why did you tear my dress Jake? I'm not a kid you can't tell me what to wear." I thought for sure he'd pop a gasket at that one. His nose flared, his fists clenched and he gritted his teeth. He pulled me into him and sat on the bed dragging me over his knees.

"You…do…not…wear…what…I tell…you…not…to... fuck." Each word was punctuated with a hard slap to my ass which was already heating up. "Jake cut it out."

There were tears because those things stung but inside I was jumping for joy. My man was back and boy was he ever. After spanking my ass he threw me face down on the bed and tore my panties down my thighs. I looked over my shoulder to see him unzipping his jeans.

"Don't you fucking move or it's gonna be your ass." I turned my head back around and bit my lip to stifle my laughter. His big hands came around my hips and he pulled just my ass up. I felt his tongue enter me from behind and started cumming immediately.

After he'd made me cum in his mouth twice he licked the red welts his hands had left on my ass before kneeling and slamming into me. I arched my back taking him deeper inside. He'd kept up his lecture but I heard about half of what he said. I was too busy enjoying the pummeling of my life. He took me all night that night, throwing me around the bed like a rag doll from one position to the next. I was a very sore but extremely happy girl after that. Suffice it to say I had my husband back and was ready to strangle him within the week.

Jake

"I have to get going boys Jacqueline's time is near and I don't like leaving her alone in the evenings." We were wrapping up the last case we'd just taken care of, human trafficking into slavery. What the fuck? We'd saved men, women and children from a fate almost certainly worst than death.

Supe was gonna have his hands full explaining to the powers that be how it was that an Op that had gone off without a hitch had culminated in the deaths of three traffickers and their boss who hadn't even been on scene.

"She's not alone I just spoke to Melissa they're all over there doing that egg thing." Shit, my fucking wife doesn't listen for shit. I distinctly remember telling her hardheaded ass not to do that shit.

She's due any day and the doc said she was carrying low whatever the fuck that meant. I understood it to mean she should be staying off her fucking feet and not running up and down painting fucking eggs. I grabbed my keys without another word and headed out of the office.

At least they waited until they thought I'd made it to the elevators before breaking into laughter. Disrespectful fucks, everyone thinks I'm over reacting about the whole pregnancy deal but I saw that morning sickness shit and what it did to her. Not to mention the horror movie the sadist at the Lamaze class deal had shown. I'd almost threatened to have her ass arrested but Jacqueline said it was perfectly natural to show a room full of pregnant women that gruesome shit. Sick fuckery if you ask me.

The baby was coming along well in her tummy, which was nice and round on her small frame. I think she looked sexy as fuck and the reaction of my dick when I walk in the house every evening and see her sitting in one of her tight tops that shows off her bump is testament to that fact. Far from curtailing our bedroom theatrics this pregnancy deal has amped things up a little.

She likes having me inside her every chance she gets and she has her sneaky little ways of getting what she wants. If I'm in my home office working on something and she gets hot she'd come in and give me a little show, which would make my cock hard enough to pound nails. Then I'd bend her over my desk and fuck the shit out of her until we were both happy and I could get back to what I was doing.

After the situation with Samuels I'd decided to take it easy on her. I gave her more leeway though it drove me insane. I'm one of those fuckers that need to possess what's mine. I needed to be in control at all times, it was the only way I could keep her safe. But I'd throttled back and given her some space. She'd put paid to that shit with the dress thing. It had taken me a few days of her walking around with the cat that ate the canary smile on her face to realize she'd played me but I let her have that one.

Samuels the fuck was in a prison infirmary in one of the worst prisons in the country. I'd pulled some strings to get that done but I didn't want him doing his time in

232 | BAD BOY

some cushy hole somewhere fuck that. For trying to fuck with my wife his ass was now mine for the rest of his miserable life.

Some days Supe swears he should've just let me kill the fuck, especially after I'd found a way to have it leaked in his new home that he was an ex cop, oops. He'd been stripped of everything by the time I was done. Now he was a non-talking cripple in a wheel chair who had no way of telling anyone who'd fucked his shit up. As long as the fuck's mind still worked I was satisfied, he should live everyday with the memory of how he got there.

Her sperm donor was another asshole I'd put behind bars. He and his band of dirty cops weren't faring much better. I'd made sure his wife got everything that was left when the smoke cleared. He wouldn't be needing t where he was and since there wasn't a snowball's chance in hell of him ever seeing the light of day again his wife and daughter had benefited. It helped that he'd built up his wealth by using his wife's inheritance in the first place the piece a shit.

So the judge had seen no problem with giving her back what was rightfully hers. Now she's under my care as well though it had taken me a minute to warm up to her. Seeing her with my wife and her excitement over my son had gone a long way to assuaging any hard feelings I'd held against her. In the end she was just one more in a long line of people whose sole purpose in life seemed to be helping my wife find new ways to send me to an early grave.

Now I have to go deal with this shit, no doubt my house would be full of women doing who knows what to the shit. She listens when she feels like it these days because I can't beat her ass and I hate giving her the cold shoulder which she seems to see as the worst of the two.

I roared my bike down the drive and parked before running up the steps. Just as I expected my house was full of people. I saw my little sneak trying to slip away while the others smiled and acted like they were supposed to be there with their shit.

"Take it next door ladies." Jacqueline peeped around the corner at me and I gave her my you're gonna get it look. "You, find a chair and park it." I pointed a finger at her; she rolled her eyes but had the good sense to obey me.

"Son we're almost done, it doesn't make sense to move everything over there now…" Mom was putting the finishing touches on an egg or some shit. Melissa was sitting Indian fashion on the floor doing the same while Linda and Mindy were putting eggs in baskets.

"Here babe I think these are the last…oh shit." You've got to be shitting me. My new brother in law of three months headed back into the kitchen with his basket of, I guess more eggs. What a sap, my sister has that poor man so whipped it's embarrassing; he's young yet, he'll learn.

"Get it moving people, mom you should know better, she has to stay off her feet." They all started talking at once, my wife my mom and hers were the loudest of the bunch. "Son it's okay women have been having babies since the beginning of time…"

"They weren't mine, she is. The doc said off her feet, beat it she doesn't need this sh…" I had to pull my shit in because my man Andrew was watching my every move and Melissa's little demon spawn was all ears.

"Melissa would you mind getting your criminal in training off my stereo? What the fu…what's he putting in there?" The kid is a true menace, he got way more of his mother than Jason that's for sure. Makes me wonder what mine's gonna be like.

My heart lurched in my chest and I looked over at her. I'm so fucking happy it's not to be believed. Everything I'd ever wanted was mine and it had turned out better than anything I could've ever imagined. I walked over to where she was now sitting and rubbed her cheek with my thumb.

"Hello Mrs. Summers." She smiled and rubbed her cheek into my palm. "Hello husband." Room full of people or not I bent my head to her and kissed her long and hard until the peanut gallery started oohing and aahing like a bunch of fifth graders. "You really want to do this baby?"

"Yes Jake it's fun and I'm not doing too much I promise." I turned back to the room at large who'd already started getting their shit together to head out. "Okay you can all stay. I'll be in my office if you need me baby."

They left her a few hours later and I ran her a bath to relax in while I took care of dinner. The mothers had offered to take over that little task for us but I'd wanted to do it, I liked taking care of my woman. She got to carry the kid the least I could do is help out around here. After I'd made sure she'd had enough to eat it was time to relax with a movie or something.

"I just wanna go to bed." I knew it, all that running around bullshit wore her out. I didn't let her know that I was pissed the fuck off just helped her up and back up the stairs.

"Lay with me Jake I wanna cuddle." I kicked off my shoes and climbed in with her wrapping my arm around her middle so I could feel little man practicing his gymnastics.

"How's he doing in there baby?" She covered my hand with hers and squeezed. "He's asleep he had a long day." I knew what she was after when she pushed her tight ass against my cock, which was already sniffing around for some action.

It never fails, just one look at her and I'm ready to fuck. I lifted my hand to her nipple and played my thumb over it until it was hard before rubbing her tummy and moving lower to her pussy through the silk panties.

Easing my fingers under the waistband I teased her clit until it was soft and slippery beneath my hand. It was an easy slip from there to the hole that hid all my treasure.

I fingered her while rubbing my cock against her ass. "Raise your hips baby." I helped her off with her underwear before pushing my jeans down my thighs. "Lift your leg as high as you can love." She lifted her legs up and back opening herself up for my cock, which I slipped inside her easily.

"Fuck, paradise." She was hotter than usual these days and my cock loved it. I held still and played with her tits until she started pushing back harder letting me know that she was ready to fuck. I slid in and out of her while latching onto her skin with my teeth.

"How is your pussy tighter fuck?" She was like a hot vice strangling my cock as I used all my self control not to thrust into her too hard. "Faster Jake I'm almost there…right there right there." Shit I know that tone my dick was in for a workout. I got to my knees so I could better control my strokes and with my hand on her hip pulled her on and off my cock.

"I wanna move Jake." Without waiting for an answer she pulled off and got on her knees. I had no choice but to fuck her doggie style the way she likes. When she tried arching her back too deep I had to take control again.

"No baby don't do that." I put my hand under the bulge of her tummy to hold her up and in place for my cock as it slid in and out of her.

"Cum baby fuck." I was so close to the edge but I knew she'd get snippy if I didn't get her off even though she uses my left over hard for a little extra. She reached down pass my hand for her clit and was soon squeezing around me. I emptied inside her with a loud growl and held still while she fucked herself on my still hard cock.

I was beat and so was she so we went to bed early that night. I've been sleeping rather light these days because I knew her time was close and I didn't want to miss anything. I felt my son tightening up in her womb a minute before she jumped up in bed.

"Jake." I was up and getting dressed before she was finished calling my name. "I know baby I felt him." I helped her get dressed while clearing my mind of everything but what was at hand.

I recited every fucking thing I'd learned in that fucked up class as I put her feet in her shoes. I called the doctor and then my mom and hers.

She hadn't made a peep so far, in fact she was acting like business as usual as she walked over to her packed bag. "Leave that baby I've got it." I grabbed her and the bag and took her down the stairs and into the garage where my truck was. Mom, Mindy and Dylan pulled out behind us and followed us to the hospital.

She started breathing heavy and clutching her stomach and I felt my first brush of fear. Don't lose your shit Summers she needs you for this. I sped through the streets and felt no shame in using the siren to get through the few late night drivers and pass red lights.

The hospital staff was waiting for us with a chair but I picked her up myself. "Jake…" Shit she was scared which was to be expected.

"It's gonna be fine baby I'm right here." I have to say the nurses were on their game. They helped me out a lot when I became all thumbs and couldn't remember shit that I was supposed to do. She kept a death grip on my hand the whole time that they were prepping her until it was time to go to delivery.

The doctor was way too chirpy for me while my fucking wife was screaming in pain. Her talk about dilations and centimeters went right the fuck over my head.

"You wanna tame it down a little? She's in pain telling her how good she's doing isn't fucking helping. And why aren't the drugs working?"

I had a long list of grievances as my wife was in stirrups screaming her lungs out and digging holes in my wrist. The doc pretty much just laughed me off as she went about her business. I kept my eyes on hers whispering to her the whole time, keeping her as calm as I could.

"He's almost here baby just push for me." She kept her eyes on mine, sweat running down her face, her hair plastered to her head and she was still the most beautiful thing I'd ever seen.

"I can't wait to see him at your breast, can't wait till he takes his first steps." I kept talking about anything that came to mind just to take her mind off the pain I was sure she was feeling.

"I see his head, one more big push and we'll meet your son." I looked down at the doc's voice and back to Jacqueline. "Go see him Jake."

"No I'm not leaving you, now push." I heard that little scream of outrage and my face broke into the biggest grin. He was raising hell already and he wasn't even a minute old yet. They cleaned him up and placed him on her chest and the love just overwhelmed me. My whole world right here. I kissed both their heads and sent up a prayer of thanks for the two of them. "Thank you precious girl he's perfect, you're perfect."

THE END

You may find the author @

Jordansilver144@gmail.com

http://jordansilver.net

https://www.facebook.com/groups/4609974
10678978/

https://www.facebook.com/MrsJordanSilver

If you enjoyed this you might also like these other works by Jordan Silver

Lyon's Heart

The Lyon Trilogy

Stryker

Stolen

Taken

And many more…

Jordan Silver is the author of thirty-five and counting novels in ebook and paperback.

Thank you for reading and I hope you enjoyed.

Made in United States
North Haven, CT
02 March 2022

16655279R10134